Vengeance

Leslie Caron

VENGEANCE

Doubleday & Company, Inc.
Garden City, New York
1982

Library of Congress Cataloging in Publication Data

Caron, Leslie
Vengeance

I. Title.
PR9105.9.C37V4 823
AACR2
ISBN 0-385-17896-4
Library of Congress Catalog Card Number 81-43630

Printed in the United States of America
First Edition

Contents

Vengeance

Foreword

Nothing in these stories is entirely truthful, yet there is an element of truth in each. Had I wanted to tell all, I would have written my memoirs, souvenirs, or what have you. But creating a face, or an event, from a small clue, giving it body and a landscape behind it, is infinitely more satisfying than the recounting of events I already know. I like to be surprised, too.

I started to write in 1967. The death of my mother, a shattering experience that caught me totally unprepared (is one ever prepared?), left me with a strange legacy. I had expected that, with time, my mother would become a faintly irritating, eccentric old lady, no more resembling the lovely perfumed woman who glittered before my childhood eyes—Our Lady of All Virtues—than the petals pressed between the leaves of a book resemble the living flower they once were. But instead of detachment, my pain deepened each time I saw her and was aware of some deterioration.

Her life had been a series of efforts toward self-expression, ambitions never fulfilled, always miscarried, stillborn —first on the stage as a dancer, later as a writer. Walking behind her, I placed each foot in her footprints, but continued where she had stopped. I became the dancer she had been for only a couple of seasons, and the actress she had wished to be. When my mother died, piles of paper scratched with her fine pencil stroke, pages and pages of incoherent notes written in an unpublishable form, were found and disposed of. I started to write the week after her tragic death, practically the day of my return from her funeral, hoping that her spirit might, through this perpetuation of her effort, find some appeasement. The same motor that propelled my mother drove me on. If I kept doggedly at my writing table, even though I was enticed by the theater or films or TV to do easier tasks, it is because for me the finest achievements are those of the pen. Having had no time to go to school because a ballet dancer's discipline rules over her childhood as well as her youth, I have kept an insatiable appetite for learning. Books! To me God the Father is a writer.

I wrote in English from the first, because I was living in England and had been for some years. Although French was my first tongue I have spoken and read English for most of my adult years. My first attempts at writing filled the wastepaper baskets. Friends were kind or polite enough not to smile when I would say, "I'm writing a script," and later, "I'm writing stories." Jean Renoir and François Truffaut were among those who kept a straight face, encouraged me, and gave advice. One day, when ready to throw in the towel, I asked Renoir at what late age one could still expect to learn a new craft. He paused awhile, then answered ruefully, "Eighty?"

When I completed my first story, intemperate arrogance overcame me. A writer friend warned, "The first one is easy. Now you must write ten more—sustaining power is what you need." I kept my nose to the paper and refused to count the pages.

These stories come from everywhere. It is not true that there are only so many stories in one's head. The difficulty is to write them all, not to dream them up.

Much as Charles-Henri did, my father would answer, when asked his name, "Claude-Chéri-Caron—*trois ans*." There are mysteries in our family which I guessed at, but which were never confirmed. My father did not reside as a child in the house in Neuilly that I describe in "Charles-Henri"—I did—but I believe the circumstances were much the same. The butler who plays the accordion is the one who taught me to ride my bicycle, and his wife, Odilia, was our maid. Severe and outspoken, she embroidered delicate pink linen shelf covers bordered with white scallops. She was queen of the backstairs world, reigning over the closets and their rich contents. Cora is only partly my mother. I have superimposed on my mother's vulnerable blond face that of a harsher woman who entered my father's life to destroy it. Evil does exist and is released when the other pole, good, loses the strength of its magnetic pull. Alcohol will do to transform a good man, a reasonable and intelligent one, into a wild killer dog. When he is out to destroy, reason cannot appease him. I refer to the Boogeyman.

The little girl in "The Cat-o'-nine-tails," Claire, is myself. The story narrates a vivid souvenir of one of my first nights in a boarding school where, thin and sickly, I was supposed to build up my health. The other little girl in "Curtain Call" is also a onetime me. I did, it is true, paint a charming portrait of this young dancer, and I ask the reader's forgiveness for this outrageous narcissism. But there comes a point when the main character in one's past ceases to be oneself and becomes just a little girl. I idealized her for the purpose of the story. Again the reader is warned: These are not my memoirs.

The girl in "Pozhaluysta" is for a while my American-born mother, who taught herself, lying on her bed amid a paraphernalia of pencils, papers, razor blades, and erasers, French, then French history, and finally Russian. Her pretext at the time—right at the end of the last world war—was that the Russians might overtake Western Europe, and "We might as well get ready," she said with foresight. She did meet a Russian taxi driver in New York, and it was arranged that he should converse with her on his time off, and I think there was a misunderstanding on his part—the rest is fiction.

"King of the Mountain" developed from a story I heard many years ago in Hollywood. Someone was invited to a party in Beverly Hills and all evening had the uncomfortable feeling of having already been in this house. Finally this person was told that this was the house of so-and-so, who had moved it from the valley after suddenly striking it rich. The guest had attended the moving party, which had lasted three nights, but had not visited the house since it had been planted in its new situation.

"Claudine Goes Home" is the most fictitious of all the stories. Years ago I read in the paper about an event that delighted me. A child, raised in London, emigrated with her family to Australia. She didn't like it there and decided to go back home to London. She used a very simple stratagem. Every time there was a ticket check, on the bus or on the plane she had elected to travel on, she would turn around and pipe up, "Mummy! Daddy! Hurry up!" It worked. She was not detected until, in London, she asked someone to call her uncle to come and fetch her. The trickery was then discovered, the press gathered. She held a press conference at London Airport. The little traveler was eight, I believe. It may be pointed out that this story has little to do with the penny dreadful I wrote. I will only say in self-defense that I had every intention of ending the story of Claudine with this delightful twist, but the beginning of the novella became so sad under my pen that the ending had to be tragic. The lucky stowaway did not fit into the picture anymore.

Of course, "George Harcourt, Touring Actor," is pure fiction, and so is "Stardom, at Last." "The Dullard" is not fiction at all. A whole family quite close to me is involved, and the secret of their identity is best kept between themselves and me.

"Vengeance," the title story, is loosely based on the life of a remarkable little woman so full of spunk that a whole book would not do her justice. She gave me a few clues about her background one day when I was admiring the fine ironing of her blouse. She then admitted that as a young girl she had worked as a laundress to pay for her studies. With a little prompting she disclosed other surprising details of her life. Her story trotted in my mind, dramatic embellishments being added with time.

Some may see a revealing clue in the choice of this story as the title one. They are right and yet again they are wrong. If I wish to cry "Vengeance" it is only against those who wanted to shelve me (as they did George Harcourt, touring actor) in a wax museum, the dust of oblivion blurring slowly the angles of my face. I dearly hope that my halloo is also accompanied with notes of humor and compassion, else I will have failed and my tune will merely be discordant.

Leslie Caron

Pozhaluysta

Margaret was the only child they had. She was a brilliant student at school. Unfortunately, her father having drifted away, gone to town for a Saturday night drink and never come back, she was taken out of school after graduation. She pursued her studies at home. History interested her, and geography, but most of all literature. She was not interested in young men, thought them boring. She was cruel to them, even, would put them through a test. "Have you read Pierre Jean Jouve? And Flannery O'Connor's short stories?" and she wanted to talk about the men in Lou Andreas-Salomé's life. "Did you read her memoirs? I love them." Of course, they were able to name every member of the Lakers, but Freud, Rilke, and Nietzsche were not among their acquaintances. They were soon discouraged.

At eighteen, she left her mother, a simple woman who couldn't understand why her husband had abandoned her, and was forever going on about it. Margaret took a part-time job typing manuscripts, which she could do at home, to pay for the dingy rooms she rented. She disguised the squalor of her bedroom by hanging the walls with sheets of a tender blue flower print. The rest of the apartment was of no interest to her.

The few young men who continued to visit her, because she had lovely brown eyes and a fine grain to her skin, soon found out there was no hope because, you see, she used to study lying down, dressed in a black silk Chinese outfit, and her bed was totally occupied with immovable bric-a-brac: books of reference with markers at the precise page, piles of paper covered with her fine writing, an assortment of erasers, pencils—her favorites were number two and she was very fussy about their sharpness, used razor blades to shape them, and those were on the bed too. The visits dwindled down and that suited her fine.

When she had read through American history, which she thought was really too short and unsophisticated for her taste, she tackled French history, infinitely more rewarding in length and ramifications. It linked her with the life of all of Europe's royalty, and this was more enriching than any living person she could have met. Only it soon became apparent that she ought to start by learning French, which would give her access to a lot more material. This took her several years, but she was never discouraged. You see, she thrived on difficulty.

Once French and French history were mastered—she was about thirty by then, her notes neatly classified in folders, according to lineage of royalty and aristocracy, legitimate and illegitimate—she felt a void in her life. She felt sure she was missing something, something truly essential. She had become aware of the joys of reading in the original and she was convinced that the Russian translations of her favorite authors were heavy-handed. She became obsessed with the necessity of learning Russian to see whether she was right or not. Now, Russian is a hard language to learn, harder yet to learn on your own, what with its large alphabet and strange sounds. But she worked diligently and in five years she felt confident that, yes, Gogol, Turgenev, Pushkin, Tolstoy, Chekhov, and Dostoevsky, were infinitely richer in the original.

Yet she felt somewhat lonely in her new knowledge. She wished she could converse with someone, exchange the thrill of those beautiful sounds, discuss the hopelessness of Russian sentimentality, the childlike fatalism that she knew was part of all the Mashas, Nikitins, Alyoshas, and others she'd met in the books.

In the solitude of her life, Margaret had taken to speaking quite freely with whomever she met in her few outings to deliver her typing or go to the grocery store.

He happened to be a taxi driver of Russian origin. Sitting in the backseat, she let on that she was going to buy Russian books. She detected a trace of accent and was so thrilled that she had to ask him what his real name was, for she could tell at a glance that the one on his license had been made up. "Yuri, that's for George, Plemianikov," was his reply. After a while the meter was stopped and through the grilled partition an exciting conversation took place. She leaned forward on her seat and her lovely brown eyes lit her face up with childlike eagerness, so anxious was she to understand and pronounce correctly. All those years of calm study had preserved her skin from wrinkles, from the lines of worry that the chaotic lives most people lead carve on their faces. She was polite, too, and considerate in her halting Russian. His, of course, was a bit rusty, because he only spoke it to his parents, and they were very old now.

Margaret, in her utmost innocence, proposed that they should meet from time to time in her apartment where all her books were, to read and converse in Russian. "It would do me so much good," she added, "to talk with a real Russian." So a day and time were agreed on, and Margaret felt a great joy in her heart.

When he rang the doorbell, it was obvious that he had washed carefully; Margaret, too, had gone to some trouble. She had bought some cleansing powder to wash the linoleum floor and wipe the shelves where all the books were lovingly displayed.

Of course, there had been a dreadful misunderstanding. The taxi driver thought she was a tease certainly, one of those coquettes who hide their game with a cunning story. But he could understand that. Why shouldn't a refined lady be a little shy at first and use a few feminine tricks? So he went along with the tea, although he would have preferred something stronger, but when she put the books down on the table he thought all this beating about the bush had gone far enough. He laughed and said, "Who cares about Russian now?" He was an American, and American was good enough for him.

Running around the table to catch her was rather fun, as a matter of fact. She escaped into the next room, which didn't have a key, because kitchens don't have keys. He didn't pay any attention to the rummaging in the drawer; the chase was so exciting that he even exaggerated the breathlessness and the grunting. He caught her by the waist next to the refrigerator and tried to find her mouth, although he was laughing so hard at her distress that his movements were a little sloppy.

When he saw the knife shining in an arc, as she was about to stab him in the back, he didn't stop laughing, he didn't get mad at all, just slapped it out of her hand, and called her "silly woman." After that she stopped fighting. He pulled her to the bed, which she had cleared for once, she wondered why at this point, and made love to her in his direct way, but not brutally. He was enjoying her plump lovely skin, directing her to turn over when it pleased him and grabbing her breasts fully in his hands. He lifted her waist and bent her backward to suck at her brown nipples and played around with her body until he couldn't restrain himself anymore. He discharged in her with a violence that frightened her.

She was still out of breath later on, long after he had slammed the door and his steps had receded down the corridor. Lying on the bed just as he had left her, many hours ago, still overwhelmed by the experience, she was unable to clear up in her mind what she thought of it. She was very disturbed, certainly. This experience had disrupted the quiet somnolence of her body, throwing her senses into bedlam, bringing chaos to the neat arrangement of her thoughts. She had felt emotion before, strong, tender emotion, but never centered in the reality of her own life. She had up till now transferred all her loving, her fears and sadness, onto the fictitious lives she read about. But this had been a great shock, an outrage that upset her, except that somewhere through the uproar of her mind fleeted from time to time the thought that something about it had been exciting, a thrilling revelation. It surprised her to realize that, together with the terror and shame, she could recollect this feeling of excitement, stronger even than when she had traced the names of the bastard children of Louis XIV with Mademoiselle de La Vallière.

She wasn't altogether a novice. She had once gone through the perfunctory act of losing her virginity and out of politeness had submitted to two more attempts at understanding what everybody made such a fuss about. But these experiences had left her totally indifferent. She had found it painful, unpleasant, and even faintly ridiculous. She had classified such incidents as "a messy waste of time" and had dismissed them from her mind.

But this had been quite different, and although she made a serious effort to clear her mind completely of what she considered now an accident, the nagging unidentified thought would float up from her subconscious, a haze, yes, a hazy emotion of great import colored strongly with fear and gripping thrill. Before she could get rid of this disturbing pang it was imperative that she identify it, but when she did she quickly closed the door to this memory, the recalling of which left her out of breath.

She went through a week of intense cleaning, washing herself carefully, her hair, her nails, her ears, even her insides, as much as she could. She drank inordinate amounts of water, which seemed called for and effective; she felt calmer afterward. She then washed or sent to the cleaner all her clothes and the small amount of household linens she had. Then she scrubbed every corner of her apartment in the most meticulous manner, after which she felt once again the sovereign of her private sphere and could confine the independent will of her body to neglect and oblivion.

All was normal again, or nearly so. Three weeks had passed, and she went back to her Russian books with renewed conviction. She could almost tell herself that she had forgotten.

It was twelve-thirty when the bell rang. She knew it because she had eaten no breakfast that morning and, feeling hungry by then, had just looked at the time. Later she couldn't, for the life of her, explain why she had opened the door, only a crack it is true, but opened it just the same, enough for him to push it, in the most natural way, while he explained his reasons. "Just to see you. I felt like dropping in just to see you."

It was too late now, he was in, and at this point she realized with disbelief that her will was unequal to his. Why so? She didn't know, but he could with easy authority modify her will to suit his desires.

She didn't fight him when he put his arm around her waist to lead her to the bed. He took her again with unhurried pleasure and assured her, as if she had asked him, that she would in time enjoy sex with him "when you let go," he told her, "when you stop believing in your goddamned female autodynamics." He then asked for food, explaining as a manner of excusing himself that he had come during his lunch hour. "Just a sandwich, see, don't go to any trouble for me." Again she bent to his will, though she resented him now that the surprise was over. She resented his matter-of-fact friendliness and told him so at the door, when, with an awkward stroke on her arm, he said, "I'll come and see you in a while, next week maybe," and he added, seeing the opposition in her whole attitude, "if you don't mind." "Yes, I do mind," she shouted; "what makes you think you have the right?" He looked at her seriously, at a loss for a few seconds, then broke into a mocking smile. "You take things too seriously. *Do svidaniya!*"

She couldn't explain it, she just couldn't explain. Why hadn't she gone to the police last time, and why had she opened the door this time? There was no excuse. Was she just stupid, or did she like fooling around with danger?

She was so outraged at her own senseless submission that she didn't go through any of the measures she had gone through last time. "Not worth it," she thought, and just concentrated on her Russian. She noticed, though, that whenever there was a description of a dashing, masculine sort of hero, the person of Yuri Plemianikov would pop into her mind and her thoughts would wander that way.

A decision is a decision. Not trusting herself farther than she could extend her arm, she had rehearsed the scene many times. "I can't . . . Go away, please. This is my . . . I am . . . I feel unwell," spoken through the locked door. "Oh," said he with a definite softening of his voice, "yeah, I see, sorry to hear that. Look, I brought you some flowers. If you want, we could just talk Russian, it's okay with me." She didn't trust him, although his voice sounded sincere. "I've brought my sandwich, I don't want to cost you nothing." She could remember the particular smell of his skin, just hearing his voice, but she kept the promise made earlier to herself. "I'm sorry. Thank you for the flowers." Her ear to the door, she listened to his heavy steps receding down the corridor. Now she felt relieved but somewhat disappointed too. But her heartbeat pounded against her temples as the steps started getting nearer again instead of diminishing down the stairway, as she had expected.

"Look, are you all right? You want I get you a doctor or something?"

"No thanks, I don't need anything."

"Okay, well, I'll come tomorrow 'n' see how y'are. So long."

She waited until she could see him, through the window, get into his cab before she opened the door to see if he had really brought her flowers. She found four roses, from his garden obviously, wrapped in aluminum foil and, inside, some damp newspaper to keep them moist.

The next morning was Wednesday; she had slept fitfully. To calm her nerves, because she found she couldn't study and might as well do something with her hands, she baked a pie as she had seen her mother do so often, but this one, being her first, didn't seem to have that professional look she had wished for.

She opened her door immediately but explained that she wasn't right yet. He said, "That's okay," and followed her into the kitchen. He had brought two sandwiches and two beers: "One's for you. I thought maybe you weren't able to go out. Want it?" They ate in silence at first, then she started to chitchat in Russian to break the embarrassed spell that seemed to have taken hold of them. He was eager to comply, laughed good-naturedly at his or her mistakes. After a while the silence fell again heavily between them. This time she spoke in English.

"Are you married?" He answered with some reticence, as if this was the cause of many problems, "Yeah, I got a wife and three kids: Liza, Ed, and Maggie," sighing deeply, as though bound by a deep-seated anguish he had tried many times to shake off. "We live in Brooklyn," he added simply.

"My name is Margaret too," she said, just to keep things going. He had trouble focusing his attention on her again. After a few seconds he smiled. "I'm not surprised, you got nice brown eyes like her."

He wanted to tell her something, she could sense it, but didn't know how to say it.

"See, after she had Maggie, my wife had those problems. They had to operate on her, she was feeling . . . she was in pain for a long time . . . she said it was my fault. Well, she don't want me since then." That was it, he had it off his chest now, he looked at her relieved, lightened of his burden of guilt, anxious for her to understand.

After that Wednesday he came regularly, twice a week, sometimes three. She accepted him now, even looking forward to his visits. Winter was here, a New York winter seen through milky-white opaque curtains, many layers of gauze filtering, softening the severe gray buildings across the street so that they would seem farther away, and she felt cocooned in her gratification. He would knock gaily in his own code and quickly peel off the layers of clothes that bundled him so he could lead her to the cozy warmth of their lovemaking. She responded now to his skillful virility, followed his lead and his timing, accompanying in harmony the supple partner swaying through a demonstration tango.

He took the time to speak Russian to her and she found that the awakening of her senses had stimulated her aptitude to learn, quickened her understanding. She became quite fluent, delighting in the intimacy both with the man and with his native tongue.

Christmas came with an exchange of small gifts. She went to visit her mother, who thought she looked quite well and rosy.

When the crisp sunny days of spring came he would stretch his lunch hour to take her for a ride in the park, just to please her. She would have sandwiches ready with pickles; he always brought the beer.

She wasn't ready for it when it happened. How could she have foreseen the abrupt break, the snapping of gentle tendrils which now organically linked her to him. The note was curt and to the point: "Dear Margaret. I'm now back from vacation. Montana was very hot but it was good for the kids. They went swimming in the river and I did some great fishing. This is to say good-bye I won't see you again, better that way. I hope you're okay. Thanks again for everything. George."

Margaret felt deserted and remembered how it had happened to her mother, who had not understood either. She kept going over and over their last hours together. One Friday he had announced the imminent vacation; just as she had expected, he was going off to Montana, wife, children, and all, to his in-laws; he would be coming back at the end of August and would drop in the next day, which would be easy for him because his family was staying back there while he had to come back to work. He had been direct about it, yes, simple and affectionate in his leavetaking. Nothing, no outburst, no changes in his comportment had ever announced that he was tired of her. So she had waited patiently from the end of August on, but had felt lonely for the first time in her life, building up a reserve of passion she didn't know existed in her. Her body, independent of her will, was literally sick from want of him, suffering more and more acute withdrawal pains as the endless days, then weeks, went by. Then one day, this short letter; she was grateful for it at least, because now she knew he wouldn't come back; but at times she thought it was just an expediency, or that his wife had found out about her and made him write it and he'd come back incessantly. There was no doubt in her mind that he liked her, needed her too; he could not have faked the pleasure he had had with her.

The bewilderment gave way to prostration: endless monotonous days stretching while her thoughts revolved round and round in the same groove. She slept badly, so put off every day the moment to get up. Months went by. She often forgot to eat and felt dizzy when she had to go down the three flights of stairs. She felt strangely ashamed, an abandoned woman, walking tentatively in the streets, so she tried to avoid going out; anyway, she couldn't stand the glances passersby and shopkeepers gave her. The grocer inquired about her health and that, too, irritated her. Why couldn't he leave her alone? No, she didn't need those vitamins, threw away the box of wheat germ he gave her when he saw the deep circles under her eyes. She had trouble reading when it was dark, and it was so often dark, perhaps because most days she forgot to pull the curtains open. She noticed that she was getting confused and forgetful in the street. Several times she thought she had seen George's taxi parked at the curb, and she was sure that she had spoken to him, only she couldn't remember if it was an hour or a month ago. One day she realized that she had nearly been run over when the screeches of brakes woke her up from her lethargy. She suddenly noticed she was in the street, not in her room. She became worried that she was being followed. There was this girl she met when she passed shop windows, always looking at her with curiosity, eyes awry in a strangely pasty face, her clothes wrinkled and mismatched, worn on an uncoordinated body. Something about that girl reminded her of herself. She stopped once and talked to her, but as the girl did the same, she became very angry, insulting her in really coarse language. A policeman took her by the arm and walked her back home. He warned her that she should get off the stuff; she did not understand what he meant.

She didn't know how this was happening, but she had trouble understanding when someone spoke to her in English. There was a strange fog in her mind, she had to slowly translate what she heard into Russian before it could make sense. This worried her: it was difficult communicating with her landlord when he came for her back rent. The man had seemed baffled by her halting English, thick with Russian accent. She tried to find the words to explain to him that she was Russian and knew only a little English. She was very concerned about this and feared that he might throw her out because she was a foreigner: she thought she must do something about it.

Tonight Margaret has reached a decision: no matter how hard and how long it will take, she will learn English, at least she'll start with the familiar words, essential for daily communication. A yellow pad in front of her, with the help of her Russian-English dictionary she writes painstakingly the Russian in the left column and the English translation in the right:

"Pozhaluysta: Please . . ."

Curtain Call

Skinny and wiry, pedaling zestfully and sweating in the July tricolor midday torpor, so that her hair is glued to her forehead—the bulk of it tied hot and heavy down her back—arrowing through the sultry heat, she can smell the green chestnut trees and, from time to time, flowers, all flower sweetnesses together—not from any town garden, but a stir of summer fragrances floating out of a flower shop. Nearing, then passing a Métro entrance or ventilation grating, she is assailed by the particular pungency which exists nowhere else in the world—the lingering memory of thousands of bodies that huddled and slept deep down on those cavernous platforms during the air-raid nights—and every normal day since, bodies hurrying off to work panting a coffee-and-croissant breath, puffing on a Gauloise or Gitane, and lately on the more fashionable American milder tobacco.

But none of these familiar scents ever reached her conscious mind. (The odors on this trail are stored away in some folded layer of her memory, to be recalled thirty years later when that incidental morning came up clearly in her mind.) Only occasionally the rumbling below-ground reminds her: "Here, right underneath me, the Métro races against me, propelled on steel tracks between Pigalle and Saint-Lazare, and I'm sure to be ahead."

But now she stops at the pastry shop where every day after ballet class she savors a double scoop of sherbet, when all at once an image freezes in her field of vision. She is struck by a new perception. Why on this particular day? Why this awareness just now? Frowning, she studies the man. Across the street, elbow gripping a flat parcel, his cigarette tipped down bitterly between tight lips, hunched slightly over the weight of some impenetrable experience of adulthood, walking with parsimony so as not to scatter his store of moral strength, a man coasts along, hugging the walls—a man with gray hair: that was how she remembered him later.

Her cone of sherbet melting near her open mouth, she tries to understand—to read what affliction, real or imaginary, has lined and aged this face. She looks around for reassurance, in the hope of erasing this photographic negative. To her stupefaction she realizes that today all men wear this gray, melancholy mask. Why? What has happened? And where are the frivolous women in flowered hats? Where are the smiling mothers hiding behind trees to play peekaboo with their tottering infants? Are there no young boys playing with their dogs anymore?

When she arrives home, enters her mother's room, she finds Madge lying on her bed. As of late, her bedspread is cluttered with volumes of the Duc de Saint-Simon's memoirs and the latest copy of *True Detective* for the more contemporary gore.

"How was ballet?" asks Madge, her mother, the voice

calmly routine, the eyes still running over the page of her book.

The girl has her back turned, facing the mirror over the mantel; she examines the new gravity on her face. How can she explain to her mother the desolation that overcame the world today, and how futile ballet seems after this tragic revelation?

The girl hears the key turn in the front door lock just as Madge says, "Here's your father, and I'm not ready for lunch yet. I must hurry."

But she doesn't. She goes on reading while the child has her eyes intently fixed on the door. Now comes the revealing instant. Now she will be able to tell from his face, recognize at once whether the same affliction has infected her father. His steps bring him near the door. He opens it.

"How was class, sweetheart?"

Her father sees her face crumple slowly and distort with pain—hot tears swell up and roll down his little girl's cheeks.

"What? What is it, honey? What is the matter?"

The child buries her face in the lapels of her father's gray suit. "There, there, honey, what is the matter?"

Madge finally lifts up her face, takes notice, is appalled at the extent of the unsuspected drama.

"My darling Min, what's the matter? Something went wrong at class?"

The child shakes her head, denying sadly. How can she articulate her distress?

"My darling, my darling, come here and tell Mama—Claude," she says with authority, "you go and set the table. I'll be right with you."

The door shut, the handle in repose, the footsteps gone

away to the far regions of the apartment, she turns to her daughter with a face so intent and concerned.

"Now, tell Mama. What is the matter, Minnie Mouse?"

The tears hotter still, filled with a grieving, a pity so overwhelming that the child feels submerged by it, never to recover youth, gaiety, or giddiness.

"I . . . I sprained my ankle," she lies, choosing this from among the more plausible explanations—also aware that this will mobilize her mother's attention.

"How, sweetheart?"

"At the barre—I fell down—Madame laughed at me; she said my legs are too thin. Oh, Mama . . . is Papa old?"

"Old, my darling? No—he's only thirty-eight—why?"

"Nothing—nothing," she repeats slowly, looking out of the window at swallows diving for low-flying mosquitoes in the sweltering heat. "But he has gray hairs, doesn't he?"

"Sweetheart, we say gray hair—in the singular. —Show me your ankle, Miss Min. Is it swollen?"

"It doesn't hurt, Mama—Mama, did Anna Pavlova have friends when she was little?"

"I don't know, darling. I doubt that she had any time for nonsense. She worked very hard to become a star." Massaging the different muscles of her child's foot: "Here? Hurts? Here?" The child shakes her head.

"Not really—it must have gone away." Unable to hide further the perplexing thing she has discovered today, or to stifle the cry of pain it has awakened: "Mama, all the men today looked sad and old in the streets. Why?"

"The men, old? Why not the women?"

"I didn't see any."

Living still with the melancholy of former days, when poverty and gray skies blended into one and the same desolation, Madge answers, "I don't know—must be this dull weather–makes everything look gray–it's going to rain again."

"But Papa looks old too, just like the others."

"Now, don't you start paying attention to failures," says Madge with pitiless logic, "in the streets or elsewhere. There are all too many of those in the world."

The weight of this immense despair will not lift. The child will not relinquish her new possession of experience: today at this hot lunchtime in her twelfth year, in her soul left innocently receptive, smilingly opened to skylarking and romping, her body always in a state of spontaneous combustion, so that Madge has to tell her twenty times a day, "Keep your legs together–pull down your skirt," the child has perceived, all in a shocked instant, the dissatisfactions, the fiascos of adulthood.

"My darling Min," says Madge, pulling her down onto her female, perfumed bed, "you mustn't worry so about grown-ups." And she wonders about this new awareness in her child, who had up till now followed obediently the course designed by her to achieve the much desired fame that had eluded her.

And so she drums into her child the marching song for child prodigies: "You must think only of your career–your future–don't you worry about sad-looking people–they're losers–you don't want to know about those." Untying the heavy, richly brown hair that spreads on the child's shoulders like a lustrous shawl: "My darling will be a great star one day and she will be young forever and have all the friends she wants–no more gray-haired men–only young men will seek you–you'll be loved and admired."

"Why don't I have friends now, Mama?"

"That's because you're working hard at becoming a star, my darling."

The child cogitates on the different facets of this problem.

"Didn't Anna Pavlova die young, Mama?"

"Of course she did, she died for her art, and her death didn't go unnoticed either. What a crowd at her funeral! But she had a long and beautiful career, all the same." And straightening her shoulders, Madge looks back at her own youth, when she herself . . . "Wherever Pavlova danced, the theater was sold out—and after the show hundreds of people would line up to get her autograph. One night, when she got into her carriage to go back to her hotel, her fans were so electrified by her performance, so wild with passion for her, that they unharnessed the horse and pulled the carriage themselves. Wherever she danced, all the little girls who wanted to become ballerinas would be brought to the theater and Anna Pavlova would judge them. She encouraged the talented—dismissed the ones who were hopeless. Thousands of mothers named their daughters after her."

A tentative knock on the door wakes Madge from her dream of glory.

"Heavens to Betsy, child," she says, gathering hurriedly her many folds of torn sweaters, pinning the top one with a safety pin tight on her shriveled breasts, patting her straw-colored locks in a futile effort at neatness, which she abandons suddenly to slip into the oldest pair of espadrilles and hurry off toward the kitchen.

After lunch, when pans and skillet and dirty dishes litter the cold stove, the child offers to wash up—hoping to learn through this inglorious task something of life's realities, which she longs to experience.

"No, my darling. You know Mama doesn't want you to ruin your hands–you can dry and put away, though." Thwarted in her attempt, the child repeats the old stratagem that may indirectly enlighten her. "Mama, tell me about Anna Pavlova's dressing room." While Madge pours hot water into two enamel basins, one for washing, the other to rinse, she sings the second verse of the aria rhythmed to synchronize the child's natural eagerness into purpose:

"Whenever Anna Pavlova traveled, the stagehands would hang white tenting on the walls of her dressing room so that every night she would find that same pristine decor. All her personal objects were spread out: silver-framed photographs–a bust of herself–facing the door, a painting of Anna in *The Dying Swan*–on the makeup table draped with white flounces, a gleaming silver tray for her makeup, her creams, pencils, and powders–and all her toe shoes, fifty pairs at least, were spread out on shelves for her to choose from. Every day, every single day, the top layer of her tutu, the silk tulle, was changed by her seamstress who traveled with her, so that when she appeared onstage you could hear the public, spellbound, exhale Ahhh! . . ." Madge, transfixed with the memory of this apparition, clasps her hands. "They were enthralled! Diaphanous she was! Impalpable–she looked as if she were gliding in from some other sphere–her pale arms were connected not to hands but to birds, in turn rising, flying, dying. Oh, the boneless flexibility of her back! She floated across the stage, fragile and light as organza."

The child was raised thus, encouraged to dream of immortality. This gray world was not for her, but an Elysium attainable only through the pain of bruised bleeding feet, aching steel-like muscles, hardened through many repeated flights and extensions, balanced precariously on an absurdly small toe. The girl complied readily with the hardships of her craft, convinced that fulfillment awaited her on her day of glory.

At last, in her sixteenth year, everyone agreed that she was now ready to be presented to the public. She had acquired exquisite grace and proportions. She, too, glided across the stage, fragile and swift as a hummingbird.

So she was engaged in the corps de ballet of the most prestigious company in Europe, and was thrilled. Not only because to dance gave her the same exhilarating omnipotence, being able to brave all laws of balance and gravity, as that of the boy who walks on a roof or a precarious ledge high above the ground, or climbs a tall tree, or does any of those improbable exploits boys will do just to live dangerously–but also because she felt she was now part of a unity, was one in an exaltation of larks, a kindle of kittens, a leap of leopards, but sometimes, too, a crash of rhinos. She was part of a group that had to link arms, support, hold, or balance each other and she looked upon her new life as the beginning of this fulfillment desired for so long.

She was rather well received by her new colleagues, though none of them had her fine grain, her allure. They forgave her because she was young and shy, unassuming even. She laughed readily when they made fun of her inexperience in worldly things. It was true that she didn't know about men or homosexuals, what went on between sheets at night, and the words used to describe these mysteries were just Greek to her. She was very impressed by those older girls, thought they knew so many things that she hadn't had a chance to learn. At home she would rave about this or that the girls had said or done, and her mother would warn her that she was not to get attached, because she was not in the corps de ballet for long. "Why?" said the girl, ashamed at being caught wanting in ambition. "This is so much fun!"

Her mother was right, the girl was fast chosen to be the star of a new ballet. She quivered with excitement and hoped secretly that she would be forgiven this defection from the ranks. Her colleagues watched the assembling, the creating of this new ballet, various degrees of bitterness altering secretly their goodwill toward her. But things were still all right so long as the public had not given sentence. The girls could still judge and advise her as they did when she was the beginner.

One day, as she was walking toward the theater for rehearsal, along streets she hadn't taken before, she stopped short in front of a cleaner's window. Sitting facing the street, exposed to prying eyes and singularly vulnerable, a girl of about her age, bent over a large fixed magnifying glass, was repairing, with the help of a small metallic crochet, the run in a fine silk stocking. Her complexion was pallid, gray circles enlarged her eyes, she frowned, and her lips were pursed with intense concentration. She raised her eyes only a few seconds, annoyed at the shadow that was blocking the light. Her gaze was not kind but scornful, stripped of any sentiment or illusion. The young dancer felt immediately guilty.

She went straight to her ballet master, and once again did not know how to explain her anguish. Did it make sense to say, "I saw a girl sitting in the cleaner's window, mending stockings—she looked so sad, and I don't want to be the star of this ballet?"

The ballet master quite rightly asked her what one thing had to do with another.

"She shouldn't do that awful job. She's the same age as I am–she has dark circles under her eyes."

"So do you. Are you suggesting that I make her the star of this ballet?" His face was severe with fury repressed. She knew his occasional bursts of tyranny, understood instinctively that he loved her and was angry with her for trying to escape from his grip; and, as each time that his desire to possess her manifested itself, usually in the form of some tyrannical remark, she gave no more access to herself, no more hold, than a flat, cold, polished slab of marble.

"I don't know," she answered, "but the girl looked at me and made me feel guilty. I don't want to be a star."

"Little girl," said the master, emphasizing the difference between their ages, "let me tell you one thing: to each according to his capacities. Do you think that this little girl mending stockings would like to have your place on the stage and hold the attention of a thousand people alone for twenty minutes? Let's go and ask her. Let's go right now," said he, his voice rising with fury, "I'm sure she'll be scared out of her wits. She'll tell you, she'd rather work from nine to six, with an hour and a half for lunch, then go to a show and watch some other girl be beautiful and clever. Now get into your tights and start rehearsing." The tone was peremptory and the young girl did what she always did: she obeyed.

The sound of applause surprised her. Naïvely, she hadn't expected it. It woke her from the most intensely adventurous suspension of time. Only an occasional cough, clearing of the throat, or creaking of a chair had made her aware, reminded her of this great watchful beast, the public, far over there in the dark hole. She had been isolated in some intensely lit privileged space, her limbs filled with the precious essence of joy, shared in complicity with her partners. And now the beast was waking up—this great single body of individual pairs of eyes—this watchful rational being, multiplied by a thousand, was expressing itself. The rainy sound of applause grew as it lasted—poured over her again and again each time the curtains rose to reveal her—it was directed to her, she knew—she could feel the heat of it—the caress of it—caress to the point of assault. She laughed and giggled with joy. So this was it—she identified it as what her mother had been describing all these years.

At last, after the great velvet pall came down for the last time, she turned around to share her laughter with her accomplices and saw the looks fixed on her. She recognized the eyes for having seen them before: that girl in the window. She tried to overcome this resistance to her happiness, to her giddiness, but a subtle no-man's-land broadened between herself and the other girls as she approached them. She was kissed and feted but with carefully restrained compliments. The joy was gone in an instant and she wanted desperately to go back to a week ago and not have to bear this new lonely burden. From now on, she would have to wait for each curtain call to feel that sweet warmth which covered her like a velvet cloak.

The Boogeyman

It had started pleasantly enough.

"You beautiful woman. La plus belle. Why do I love you so much?"

"Yes, why?" she asked, teasing him gently.

"I don't know, many reasons. You are gay, you bring me joy, you give me peace, you love me, you admire me, I guess. You are the reason I bother to go to bed every night . . ."

Every morning, she thought; not before sunrise.

". . . the reason I bother to wake up . . ."

Yes, every afternoon, as close to sundown as possible, she told herself, guilty to voice such thoughts, even privately.

"You are as necessary to me as the air I breathe."

Nicely expressed. Stavos felt pleased with himself, took a sip of his shimmering whiskey, moved closer on the couch, put his arms around her to massage just the spot between her shoulder blades where she always felt tense: his own infallible secret of seduction. Immediately her body yielded, reached toward his warmth as the flexible sweet pea leans toward the sun. But she knew that she had better check herself. It was no use trying her femaleness on him; experience had taught her that he was not interested. At this hour of the night only his ice-cube-clanking glass mattered to him.

"My little bird," he said in a misleading outburst of loving.

Not that he was often aroused. When he woke up around two in the afternoon or later, he usually felt so sick that he either barked abusive insults or else clowned pitifully. Only once in a while did he wake up with zest for life and invite her to explore the reason why between his sheets. But on most days she knew that he was feeling bad, or soon would be. His breath told her so, fetid breath spewing fumes of undigested alcohol, the hot liquid still burning his stomach, scouring the complex coursing of his veins. He woke up every day amazed to be still alive—"Oh shit, what is this joke?"—and would try, guilt helping, to organize some semblance of coherence in his mind before calling her. Three or four cigarettes, two aspirins with vitamin C, and later one of those effervescent tablets for the liver, more cigarettes in between; he called her only when he felt better.

Now he was pouring himself a third or fourth whiskey, not pretending anymore; this was an honest tumblerful.

"Oh, Stavos," she pleaded, immediately stopped by his Peking-Opera-dragon eyes.

"'Oh, Stavos,' what?" he roared. "I know what I'm doing. Get off me."

He loved the sound of the burbling liquid, pouring rich amber into the crystal glass, topped with crackling ice cubes, so that the fiery liquid would reach his stomach still cool, and at last the elaborate structure of his thoughts, his vision of things, would expand in the fertile field of his brain, not limited to dull reason anymore; every thought now developed, demonstrated, unraveled with splendidly irrational logic.

She could feel the hour of devilry coming, when one cloven-hoofed demon she didn't know the name of would take possession of him and dictate the malice he would show toward her, the monstrous shape stalking close, waiting to assume Stavos' likeness to better spring on her. It was wiser for her to hide in bed, to escape through sleep the possible aggressions of this night.

"Getting sleepy. Perhaps I should go to bed," she said, faking a yawn, trying to sound casual.

"Bed, you only have that in mind," he said bitterly, "fill your stomach and then off to bed like the shopkeeper around the corner. At least he has a reason, he has to get up at five to collect his fruits and vegetables. But you? Why can't you keep me company, talk with me?"

Have a drink, you mean, her inner voice murmured.

"It's only one o'clock, the beginning of the rich hours. When the businessman goes to sleep to dream of adding a digit to his numbered account, and the shopkeeper hears his cash register ring like a Las Vegas one-arm bandit that's come up with the three cherries, you want me to stand alone and try to comprehend the whys and wherefores, so well concealed during the routine of the day. How can I, when the upright citizen showers, eats, shops, talks drivel on the phone, how can I understand or resolve the problems of humanity? How can I, when the concierge rings the doorbell to come and vacuum the apartment, think up an unique plot for my next novel?"

He paused, waiting to see the effect of his oratory, then

took a good swill to wet his lips in case she needed other enticements.

"Darling," she said tentatively, "don't you think that you work better alone?"

He tried to attack her from another angle.

"What about staying up with me for the pleasure of hearing the garbage truck empty this street of its dainty cellophane-wrapped bundles of rich people's refuse, which haven't got enough shit in them to feed a rat; yes, poorer than poor people's refuse, because the rich give their garbage to eat to their servants who live on the sixth floor. Here garbage goes up to the attic before coming down onto the sidewalk." He was rather pleased with this image, took a long swig, emptying his glass this time. "Garbage men need our courtesy and solidarity to carry on. Hats off to the 6 A.M. effort to clean away the mess of the rich."

Yes, that should have convinced her, he thought with confidence, but decided that his bladder was painfully full, which would soon impair his imaginative powers. As he looked at the mirrored doors of the drawing room, his brain told him clearly enough that there were three doors from here to the bathroom, probably all shut, whereas the tall window to the balcony was temptingly open. Courageously resolved to brave the upholders of urban laws of decency, he walked the distance from couch to balcony with senatorial importance. A swift glance right and left to check that the street was safely empty, his left heel securely braced against the wall, a necessary precaution when you think of the well-known treachery of Newton's law, he unzipped his fly and projected the excess fluid in an artistically controlled arc, aimed at the roof of an expensive Mercedes parked there just to provoke him.

He went back in feeling much better, ready to renew

the interrupted thread of his monologue, but she was gone. He didn't feel especially defeated at having lost the battle. It was the same every night. He lit a Gitane and replenished his glass. "She will be undressing, no need to hurry. I'll go in later to tuck her in, see that she's comfortable."

The light tinkle of his glass announced him. He slid through the doorway. Claire put down her book, smiled while consolidating her inner defenses. What was it going to be tonight? Grabbing an ashtray to legalize his territorial right to this bed and establish the minimum time of his visit, the smoking of a cigarette, he now crept across the bed, examining her closely, lying in wait for her. She waited too. Suddenly his face lit up with a winning smile, the almost feminine, coquettish smile that so many women had believed in. It still worked sometimes.

"So you leave me alone to sail through the perilous night, a solitary navigator, forced to keep my arms locked on the helm while my eye is fixed on the North Star so that I won't drift and wreck my ship on some ghostly, abyssal rock?" A gesture to infinity accompanied this colorful declamation.

Claire's defense against Stavos' seduction was usually straightforward attack.

"I want to read," she said with simplicity. She chuckled at her audacity before adding, "Anything to avoid work, huh?"

He looked at her eyes, vulnerable behind the reading glasses, an aging little girl's face, stubborn and strong, although he knew her to swing precariously between resilience and extreme fragility.

The retort wasn't coming. He decided to let it go for this once.

"Do you like the book I gave you?" He was marking time.

"Yes, I love it," she said, guarded. And then, moved as usual by his look of total sincerity, love unrequited: "Thank you, Stavos."

Good, he had made a point. He puffed on his cigarette and took a long swill of whiskey. He now rubbed his chest with the right expression of pain, and breathed as if oppressed.

"What is it, Stav, do you have a pain?"

"Yes, as usual," he said darkly. "My breast is ready to explode, my heart wants to break out, my throat feels as tight as if a steel collar were constricting it."

She sighed, bored. Was she having to go through that lamentable pretense again? What could she say that every doctor hadn't said already?

"You know you smoke too much," she said wearily.

He suddenly turned his full attention on her.

"A psychiatrist once told me: 'You're a trapeze artist who throws himself through life without a net.' I fly without a net," he said with evident satisfaction.

Yes, she thought, looking at him blandly, without a net, but someone has to stand under you, arms open, and when you fall, you kill.

"Stav, I'd like to read," she said patiently.

"Yes, yes, let me finish this cigarette. Can't you let me finish this cigarette?" He scowled, showing the one he had just lit to extend his visiting visa. He looked down at the counterpane, an awkward silence setting in now that he had won his reprieve. He felt so guilty, he could almost feel the pain she was going through tonight, not much different from last night's, every other night's for years now; for so long in fact, that she hardly ever complained anymore. All the same, he knew that she would have liked him to come to bed with her, "not necessarily to make love," she had explained long ago, but for companionship, to talk, to read together, to have someone to say good night to before turning off the light. "You only slept through the night with me once in four years, and that was because you were so broken up after your car accident that you couldn't get up." Yes, even on their first night together, he had run away right after the cigarette. He just hated anything that looked like "married-couple bullshit." Couldn't she understand that? Sleeping and making love with her had nothing to do with loving her. The proof was that on those long vigils alone with his bottle of whiskey he had to check that she was there, in their bed. Every time he went to the kitchen for ice and passed in front of the bedroom, he would push open the door and stand in the dark doorway listening to her breathing. Sometimes she slept so deeply that she even snored a little. That was usually when she had taken too strong a sleeping pill. She used to tell him, "We're a pretty sad couple: you spend the night with your bottle, while I sleep with a pill." Once she had asked, "Do you drink because you don't want to make love to me and you know I won't ask you to come to bed if you're drunk enough? Or is it that you don't feel like it when you are drunk?" He had been incapable of answering, so had told her the first thing that had come to his mind. "Neither. I want to write, that's what torments me at night. I know I can't write what is in me. I try, all night long I try. I look for ideas. Alcohol gives me ideas. Do you understand?" He had other answers as well, interchangeable. "I can't make love to you because I don't have any money. That upsets me more than you know, my little one."

Once he had said, "It's because I feel I don't deserve you." She had denied this, saying, "You fought to have me, you felt sure enough of yourself to make me break up my marriage." "Yes," he would say sadly, "you know me, I'm a chicken thief." "You mean you made me divorce just to see if you could do it, only to flex your muscles?"

But she didn't complain anymore, didn't ask for anything. She knew it was useless. Life was just an infinite bleak expanse of hopelessness now. The fight had been worn out of her. She just wanted him to leave her alone to read, to take a pill, and forget.

His cigarette was half burned, he looked at her piteously.

"You'd like me to leave you now?"

She was thinking, Oh, God, go away with your filthy cigarette. Go back in there and get drunk where I can't see you. I can't stand for you to feel all the sorrows of the world, this late in the night.

She heard herself burst out: "Stav, it's two-thirty in the morning. I got up early today. I bought the milk and the bread. I took your boots to be mended. I answered all the mail, paid the bills, saw to it that your shirts are neatly piled in the closet, clean, and all the buttons sewed on. There is a new tube of toothpaste on the bathroom sink. Bella called, we're having dinner with her and Jamie on Thursday: he has a new job. The dinner tonight was good. I loved going to the Balzar, they have a real sense of social justice there, you have to wait your turn for a table, no cheating possible. But those two Americans gave me the willies. She drinks, I'm sure of it. There is a grieving in her which he cannot heal, even though he spends twenty-four hours of each day, yes, even his nights, watching over her. And the more one drinks, the more one goes down into despair. Don't you know that? Go away, Stavos, go away. The day has been long enough, I've earned my peace, I want to forget you."

Some of it she said aloud, some she didn't. She yawned discreetly.

"You are sleepy?" he asked anxiously.

"Yes, I am sleepy."

"Are you going to sleep?"

"Yes, yes. I'll just read one more page and turn off the light."

"I'll leave you, then. I won't be long. I'll be with you in twenty minutes," he lied, "forty at the most."

She smiled sweetly. Why do you bother to pretend? she thought. He hugged her and kissed her hair with enough passion for a long good-bye before a trip across the ocean.

"Yes, don't be long," she murmured, desolate.

She waited for the door of the living room to close before tiptoeing to the bathroom to take a tranquilizer. She flushed the toilet, just in case he was eavesdropping.

Back in bed, she heard the floorboard creak in the corridor and a second later recognized the sucking sound of the icebox door being opened. And now she could hear the ice cubes being fractured out of their tray. She anticipated his steps back again in front of the bedroom door, less steady at this hour. By now she could identify even in his most stealthy night prowlings just how much he'd had. A second of fear lest he should come in again. Yes, he couldn't resist it.

"Good night, my feather-bird. I love you so much. I only came in to see if you were all right," he said with immense longing, needing her so much that she couldn't bear it.

"Yes, I'm fine, I'm going to sleep now."

"Good night, then." He tried to give her a good smile, full of the assurance of his protection, but it looked more like a hopeless prayer.

She slept fretfully; the tranquilizer kept her in some hypnotic unreality where the sketch of a dream tried repeatedly to impose itself, just as three notes out of a tune can tease one for hours, until some buzzing sound, which at first took an odd shape in her phantasmic lethargy but finally reached some level of her mind still alert, told her there was danger, something taking form, an undisclosed threat, a yawning chasm, a gap in the serene benevolence of the night, threatening to engulf them both. Murmurs, at first indistinct, unlocated, warned her; she forced her will to wakefulness. Her hand reached for the light and she sensed that the blue and white bedroom had lost its innocence. Four o'clock in the morning and malevolence was casting shadows at every angle.

Pillow-disheveled, vulnerable as one is when reality is so ill defined, Claire tiptoed to the living room. The murmur grew and became distinct as she came closer to the glass doors. She found Stavos naked except for his shorts, his clothes strewn around the room in furious disorder. Sitting cross-legged on the floor like a Jewish tailor, he was addressing someone with harsh severity. As she saw no one else in the room, it took her a while to understand who this polemic was being argued with. And then she heard the name. Logical, severe, and authoritative, but with some grandeur and nobility to add weight to his arguments, Stavos was apostrophizing an absent and unsuspecting Prime Minister. Yes, her love-sick child, her most tender concern, was dressing down the honorable Prime Minister. When he finished his side of the altercation, he listened with impatience to a defense audible to him alone; an astute drag on his cigarette, a cunning swallow of whiskey while his eyes were narrowly scrutinizing his ghostly adversary, and he was ready to attack him once again.

Fearful and guilty, hoping that her indiscretion had not been noticed, Claire slipped stealthily back into her bed, quickly turned off the light. Hugging herself in a fetal position, she hoped sleep would again save her from the howls of the wolf. She slept and dreamed of his kindness, of the first time he had kissed her, right there in the courtyard, after taking her home from dinner, and she had fainted in his arms, overwhelmed by a sweet but fearful emotion; dreamed of their early games when, the radio oozing a suave tango, he would grab her waist and swirl her dizzy, and of the day he had washed her hair with the hands of a mother careful not to break the tender membrane of the fontanel; dreamed of the first awkward days when they had moved in together and good manners and tenderness had dictated the niceties: "Would you mind if I used this shelf?—No, no—Please tell me which one you would prefer—No, you tell first." Happy days. She slept until nine o'clock.

She woke up surprised not to find his massive presence in the bed beside her; but as he would sometimes finish off the night sprawled naked on the white wool carpet of the living room, she suspected no malice, saw no threat in the blue light pouring into the white room.

Shreds of sleep enveloping her still, she went toward the living room looking for him, and there she found Satan. His eyes burning with evil, his powerful body charged with the monstrous energy built up during those long hours of drinking, he was swinging slowly on a stool, rolling his shoulders right and left, his elbows deeply embedded in his knees, a dangerous beast ready to pounce, to perform the final act, to destroy her.

"Hello, Stavos, what's wrong?" she said, trying to sound normal. "Why didn't you go to bed?"

"You are spying on me!" he roared thickly. "Stop watching over me! You've put water in my whiskey and thrown the good stuff away when my back was turned. Answer me!"

The next moment was the dead pause in the flight of a bird before plunging toward its prey. They stared at each other in silence, each trying to predict the immediate future, to outwit the other. She knew that so long as he held the stare she should not run. But her fear was such that she did the thing she must not do. Without lowering her eyes, she backed imperceptibly away, giving him who waited for a detonator to blast off his anger, the signal to attack. He got up and started toward her, roaring mightily.

"That's for trying to stifle me!" as he grabbed a lamp and threw it on the floor. "You want to make a mensh out of me!" And he kicked viciously a stack of pastel portraits, splitting the glass into a spider web of crystal. "You're like a schoolteacher trying to reform me! Leave me alone!" he yelled as he kicked again and threw on the floor and disemboweled and tore paintings, chairs, tables, books, beautiful objects, reminders of fugitive moments together, photographs of a mischievous smile, flowers, the water gurgling on the carpet among the debris; his anger feeding upon itself, in his paroxysm of rage he destroyed all.

He found her in the bedroom where she had retreated panting with terror.

"Don't," she said forcefully. "Don't, they'll put you in jail, Stav, don't!"

He still marched on her, inwardly amazed and delighted at his easy domination over this woman, usually so independent. He marched toward her, his arms outstretched as he had seen King Kong do in films, grabbed her by the throat, and pinned her down on the bed. Trembling, she warned him again of the consequences of his violence.

"Don't, Stav, don't! They'll put you in jail if you kill me, don't!"

He lifted his thick fist and hit her once, enjoying the softness of her flesh, pleased at the red mark he was leaving on her face, excited also by the mouth wide open, shrieking like an animal about to be slaughtered. He lifted his fist again. The hand came down, hitting savagely, slapping back and forth, back and forth at the face, neck, and shoulders, inflicting unbearable outrage and pain on the precious being he loved most in the world.

The devil was making love to his creature.

King of the Mountain

"There it is! Jesus! I don't believe it!"

Rachel looked up in awe at the huge house glittering like an obese jewel, every window incandescent with light, rolling, moonstruck and demented, down the whole width of the street, pulled by an absurdly small, a lilliputian tractor. The house tottered forward, wobbling on its platform, an enormous jellied dessert served on wheels. The paint was faded and peeling in places, but time, neglect, and smog had not yet eaten away the mock-Gothic confusion of turrets, balconets, and laced eaves and peekaboo windowpanes and heaven-kissing steeple waving a quixotic weathercock at the night. For a minute Rachel was speechless as the grotesque folly towered closer above the car.

"Honk, honk!"

"Rachel is here! Rachel and Phil are here!"

"They found us—great! Get one of the parking boys to help them. Where are they all!"

"Has she got slacks to climb aboard?" shouted Kitty excitedly.

Pale and blond, Rachel's face framed by curls thick as an aboriginal's wedding headdress appeared through the car window. A long arm waved. The beige-nailed hand fluttered commandingly.

"Hi, you guys! Wow, what a sight! Right in the middle of Third Street! What a house! A.C., can I reserve the Frankenstein suite for the weekend? Darling, what do we do now!"

Quiet up to now, her husband Phil leaned his head out of the driver's window. He contemplated the huge, incongruous old house, moving illogically in the middle of the street at about four miles an hour.

"Don't drive this house any faster or you'll get a ticket! Jesus, I can't believe it! Hey, A.C., where can I find one, size eight, for Rachel's birthday?"

Rachel shrieked with him, "I want one! I want one!"

Someone leaning out of a flounced window yelled, "Charles Addams slept in this very room before going spooks!"

"Yeah," yelled another face which appeared from a Gothic turret. "And I just found his jar of poison cookies!"

Out of every window faces materialized long enough for the swift barb of a joke, the ensuing outburst of laughter, while disco music blared out, throbbing against the wrinkled old walls right in the middle of Third Street. It was only ten o'clock of a balmy evening and, summoned by the laughter and the music, neighbors gathered on their front lawns, all agog to see the old house on its way to Beverly Hills—"What a circus, A. C. Weston is moving house—and no kidding!"

"Come and have a drink on the house!" A.C. offered genially. "You are all invited!"

So the neighbors, drinks in hand, walked alongside the house or went inside for a look-see.

But now A.C. came downstairs through the colored-glass front door, walked along the moving platform, smiling calmly—A.C. was always calm—toward the maroon Rolls, to greet Rachel and Phil.

"Come on, sweethearts," he welcomed, "come on in for the glorious ride to Beverly Hills. Come on in and have a drink! Here," he said to a handsomely coiffed young man in a red spencer, "what's your name?"

"Jeff, sir. Good evening, Miss Leighton," the young man emphasized as he discovered Rachel. Ignored, her husband was peeved, although accustomed to being overlooked.

"Right. Jeff will give you a claim check. He'll park your car on Camden Drive—you ask for it anytime you want. We've got ten boys with a car each. And, Rachel, anytime one of you girls wants to powder your nose, there are portables upstairs and a maid in attendance. She's got an iron and hot rollers plugged in."

"A.C., you thought of everything. How clever!"

"Well, that's Kitty really. She said she wanted a maid and the whole shmear. I'm here to tell you we've got not one but two generators. We could be shooting a film, we're using so much power. Everyone in the street is invited for a drink, and that could mean a lot of ice cubes."

"Well, I got to see this beaut for myself," said Rachel.

So Phil and Rachel abandoned their car to the attendant, who drove it off with a screech of tires, eager to show that he'd handled many Rollses already that evening.

A. C. Weston guided Rachel up the platform to the front door of the slowly moving house.

"Kitty will give you a drink and show you the place. You know everybody, I'm sure."

He stayed outside with Phil and a few of the guys who were already walking alongside the house in their immaculately polished Gucci loafers, which would never go to the shoe mender's because no one ever walked enough to wear out a pair of soles in Beverly Hills. A.C. put his arm around Phil's shoulders—he knew that one day he might want to use Rachel in one of his films—and heard himself go through the statistics yet once more.

"You wouldn't believe it, Phil, it took two weeks to get the house ready to move. They reinforced it here and there, cut the wires, cut the plumbing, all that, then they jacked it up on the platform. You shoulda seen the house creaking up inch by inch. I tell ya, soon they'll be able to fly them."

Phil was impressed.

"How long will it take you to drive it to Beverly Hills?" He had to shout to be heard above the music.

"Three nights. They'll park it during the day in an empty lot or a large corner and then off again tomorrow night at 9 P.M., when the traffic has died down. You see, Phil," he said, giving him the full privilege of his confidence, "they got quite a ways to go. For one thing, that house needs large streets; for another, the guys must avoid hills—going up is one thing, it's coming down that's the tough one."

A.C. felt so tired. He thought about this mammoth house he'd bought and the cost to fix it—this party—why had he thrown this party? To convince everyone that he was the most successful producer/director in Hollywood?

Or to convince Kitty? He thought with nostalgia of the days when throwing a party meant just drinking California wine in old pickle jars with the guys while the girls cooked spaghetti and meatballs. He wondered if his jitters showed. No, I guess they can't see me shaking. Jesus, I need a sniff—why doesn't Larry turn up? Is he trying to tell me something? Would he really dry up the cash flow? Goddammit, I need those retakes—the son of a bitch said it was the greatest thing he'd ever seen—even though it is too long—so what's wrong with *Gone With the Wind*? Nothing. Right?

Phil jarred him from his troubled thoughts.

"How much does it cost you to move the house?"

A.C. wasn't surprised at the direct question. Everyone always asked "How much?" here. No one was too big to talk numbers.

"Twice as much as the house cost and only half of what Kitty's going to spend on fixing it up. In other words, almost as much as this film I'm making. This is some production, kid."

"Yeah, I'm not surprised. But you're a lucky man, A.C. That's a great house."

"Well, I want my girl to be happy. You know what I mean, Phil?"

"Sure, A.C." Phil knew that he was referring to the dreaded disease that seemed to be hitting so many of the Hollywood women. Kitty had had an operation and was still being treated. Phil wondered why these women seemed to be particularly vulnerable when they were so well cared for and never exerted themselves. He thought he had better change the subject.

"How's the cutting going, A.C.? Doing some retakes, I hear?"

A.C. didn't show his annoyance. But he thought: That's it, right on cue. I'd like to sock him in the jaw—pow! with a right! Why can't he wait to see it at the Guild when I show it for the Academy Awards? He smiled patiently.

"Fine, Phil, just fine. It's going to be a great film." He had to affirm this with enough authority to convince those other guys who were now coming within earshot. Normal. Everyone always wanted to hear the latest about a big production that's been kept very hush-hush.

"That's what I hear," and Phil was nodding and smiling broadly while recalling that he'd heard from the cutting department that the mammoth production was long and slow. The rumor was that A. C. Weston didn't know how to end his film and had asked the studio for another month of shooting, about a third of the picture in retakes. Crazy.

"Three and a half hours of pure magic. Right?" said Phil and he nodded again.

"Yeah, I know it," answered A.C. candidly. He heard his partner, Jerry, boast to two fellows who had been trying to get their project off the ground for months and were eager for any tidbits from those who were actually in production. "What's it like being right up there, talking to the gods every day?" they were asking.

"See," Jerry was saying with false modesty, "I told Larry—only five million more and you got a wanna-see picture—not just a little peep show for the eggheads—Larry agrees—he knows—the public wants spectacles, we'll give them the biggest spectacle since the parting of the Red Sea."

Jerry should shut his big mouth. It was bad luck to discuss a project before all the green lights were on. A.C. slapped Phil's shoulder a little too hard.

"Hey, Phil, this is a party. Can I give you a drink? Here

I am, keeping you on the sidewalk, without a glass in your hand even. Want to visit the house?"

"No hurry."

The fellows were sticking around all eager to hear a word from the great man himself. "No hurry," Phil repeated, strengthened by the numbers around him. "Tell me, how's that French girl . . . what's her name . . . ? Great, is she?"

"Yeah, great," said A.C. with conviction. "Nicole Vincent. I tell ya, those French girls . . . they got it all in the kisser . . . charm"—and then, as if to confirm his appraisal of her—"she's in there. You got to meet her."

They looked toward the house, which had moved on, a noisy ship lolling away on choppy seas, and could see the silhouettes, wiggling to the beat of the music with application and self-conscious indifference, catching rays from the spotlights fixed between ceiling and floor, just for the party.

Rachel spotted that new French star immediately she came in. She thought that the blond girl looked rather mousy, even though she was ready to concede that there was something sexy in the girl's simple grooming. "These European girls play it down so much, they blend in with the wallpaper. . . ." She pretended not to see the younger girl. She had to make her entrance first. Rachel knew how to behave like a star. Let Kitty bring her to me, she thought.

With professional good grace, like a queen greeting the amateur theatrical troupe in a girls' public school, Rachel kissed a few guests, waved to others. Then Jeremy, the star kisser, came toward her, swagging one fat hip after the other in an almost oriental dance. She answered the eager questions with courageous sighs.

"Tired, real tired—oh yeah, so thrilled with the picture—soon over, thank God—I'll be glad when I can put on my jeans and cook dinner." She giggled, knowing that she was putting Jeremy on. No one really believed her housewife act.

She looked at these girls around her: executive wife types or hopeful players, or both, showing their three-ballet-classes-a-week figures in tight jeans, their puberty breasts just visible through something lacy or silky, drinking white wine because white wine isn't really drinking, or even Perrier if they were stoned, and Rachel felt a piercing envy, knowing that she was overweight—even at the end of the film—but then she remembered that she was the greatest female star—way up there where no spaceship could reach her, the only one here who could command three million per.

"Do you know Sally?"

"Sure I know Sally. Hi there, sweetums! What do you say about this house? Isn't it a gas?"

"The greatest thing on wheels since Noah's ark—I'm not seasick anymore: all you need is a stiff drink and the boat stops rocking."

Sally was putting on her outdoor-girl act, as if she didn't sniff coke just like everyone else.

"Jack and I are here to put this deal together and then back to Big Sur. Jesus, I can't stand it here—all the pressure. I miss my pets. Jack and I are raising lions, did you know?"

"Isn't it rather dangerous? Your face . . . ?"

"No, not really. They follow me around the house."

That sort of thing. Rachel insisted that Kitty show her the house. And because she was the star she was, Kitty gave her the grand tour.

"The guest room and changing room—the exercise room with Greek sunken bath. We'll make it into an indoor Jacuzzi—I counted nineteen rooms, A.C. says sixteen: the three extra ones are just walk-in closets. A Chicago stockyard millionaire built it in 1891."

"How many bathrooms?"

"Eight. All the original tiles."

"How many staircases?"

Kitty looked up at the ceiling and counted on her fingers.

"Two side towers, plus the main, plus the service stairs in the back—that's four."

"Wow, Kitty!"

"Ask me how many fireplaces?"

"How many fireplaces?"

"Twelve." There was a significant silence. At last Rachel said, "Jesus, Kitty, this is bliss."

"That's what I said to A.C. when I first saw the house. I thought I was going to freak out when he said, 'Let's buy it!'"

Rachel felt sorry for her. Of course, A.C. had bought Kitty the house because of her operation—or was it because A.C. wasn't sure of her anymore? Rachel watched her closely for signs. People said she was going to be all right, she had been caught in time. A strange girl, Kitty—no one really knew her. Rachel remembered her, way back when she was married to Enrico—frail and blond as a unisex angel, she agreed with everything her husband did or said, and smiled a lot. She smiled just as much when she was married to Frank and again now that she was married to A. C. Weston. Once in a while you heard in hushed tones that she had taken too many pills. Were these attempts? No one knew for sure. But you never saw her unhappy. Even when she found out that she had to have an operation, she kept on smiling. All through the years, you could never guess that there was trouble in any of her marriages. She never let on. One day you saw her tenderly hugging Enrico's arm, the next time she would already be with Frank and she would say, "I'm marrying Frank as soon as I get a divorce from Enrico." A couple of years' time and A. C. Weston was holding her hand. She would say, "I'm marrying A.C. as soon as I get a divorce from Frank." She was on the go all right. You couldn't catch her between husbands, and every time she was the same supportive little wife, which made the husband of the moment hope, although he must have known deep down that she was only passing through, that she would remain because he, at last, had the power to make her happy. Rachel wondered if there was a link between those repeated divorces and this malignant tumor that had festered inside her, gnawing at her flesh underneath the pretty contentment.

Suddenly the door opened: A.C. was standing there, sure of himself.

"Honey," he said, as he thought he caught a flash of hostility in his wife's eyes before she could correct herself and smile. "Larry and June are here, I need you to greet them."

He smiled at Rachel. "Did I treat my wife to a great house? What do you say?"

Rachel smiled broadly. "A.C., like everyone says, you're a genius—and what's more, you're a pretty nice guy."

The three of them went downstairs to join in the raucous melee and to greet Larry, the top guy.

Just one hour later, at eleven forty-five, Larry and June were ready to leave. They stepped down from the platform, June standing in her ballet slippers, not too close to her husband, so as not to let on that she was a foot taller. Larry then repeated, "This is a great house, kid."

After giving his claim check to one of the boys and while waiting for his car, he gave his appraisal: "A.C., you've done it again," and slapped him on the back. "I said to June only this afternoon, 'You know something about A.C.?' She said, 'What's that, honey?' I said, 'He always surprises me'—you surprised me a lot when you said, 'I need five million more to finish this picture'—after all, I been generous to you on this film. Right?—and now you surprise me with this house—I say to myself, 'This is a great house all right—I must've been generous for A.C. to afford to buy such a nice place and then to move it to a better neighborhood—and I'm glad for him'—A.C., it makes me real happy. . . . Just one thing: Is it good business? I mean, will you get your money back? It's not enough to get a great idea, it's got to be good business. Sometimes things get away from you—they cost too damn much—you know what I mean? Now, watch out, kid, or your house will run away from you." He hugged Kitty, who was standing there smiling. "Good night, honey," and he stepped into his car, which had been brought to his elbow. His eyes fixed forward, he handed a twenty-dollar bill to the young man in the red spencer and started his car without another glance at A. C. Weston.

So this was it. He was fired. It was clear enough. The boss had made up his mind, probably given the order already. A.C. knew just how things would go. Tomorrow he would turn up at the studio a bit late—say, ten. His cutting room would be locked up. He would go to the next room, where he'd be told that Joe, his cutter, had been called to the head office. He'd go there to find out that Joe had been given the day off. Larry's secretary would stop him going into the boss's office: "Mr. Finkel is in a meeting just now, but he gave me a message for you. I was just trying to reach you. He said it was best to cancel next week's shooting until he could think about it. He'll see you Friday or Monday after he's looked at the footage." Then on Monday, Larry would be unreachable. "Didn't he tell you that he was going to New York?" his secretary would murmur, surprised. A.C. would finally call his lawyer, and so on. . . . He knew how the hatchet fell, all right.

What do I do now? Put a bullet through my brain? He just couldn't live this minute, or the next—he had to do something.

First he got stoned. One of the guys at the party had some stuff. He felt good for half an hour and then his worry came back. The edges of his frustration just got keener, more vivid. He decided to look for a friend. Who in this noisy crowd could he talk to? He went to Robert, the hired butler, whom A.C. knew from practically every party he had ever gone to.

"A Coke, Mr. Weston?" Robert knew everyone's vice.

A.C. looked out of a window. They were driving past the tennis club where Pancho Gonzales had so often refused to lose the game. What was going to happen to him? This house, which was bought to crown him King of the Mountain, was running him downhill to bog him down in the flat compound of Beverly Hills, where so many sat waiting for their luck to return, more and more neglected each year.

Across the room he saw Jacques and Régine and could sense the hell they had lived together in their thirty-five years of married life. An undeclared hatred for each other had left one deaf and the other shriveled and embittered. Their son was dead—had killed himself like so many sons—so that now she starved herself in self-immolation to keep reminding Jacques of his failure as a father and a husband. A.C. didn't want to see them. He walked past Sam, the funny man, who talked one long stream of jokes—Sam was surrounded by girls.

"I don't see why you can't drive me home, A.C. I'm only a couple of blocks east of you. Is that too much to ask? Hey, come on! Listen, I know a great dog's kennel, downtown L.A. For a thousand dollars I'll roll it to your backyard and give a great party for your dog and mine—what do you say?" All the girls laughed, and A.C. saw something pointed in the joke. Sam had sized him up.

A.C. looked around at all the faces he knew, but wondered if there was one friend in the whole bunch. He saw Jeremy holding court, spread over three chairs, two to sit his affable flesh on and one in front of him to lean on. Jeremy was saying, "I heard he's shooting two endings—one for the Jews, one for the Gentiles." A.C. walked away, uncomfortable. Jeremy was poison ivy. A.C. envied him, though. His obesity had been the solution for him. Through his thick tinted glasses, Jeremy saw the world with rotund deformity. He was on the up and up at the moment. Those happy roller-skating movies might be stuffed with every old chestnut in the larder but they worked with the public. When I grew up in this community all the producers wore glasses to look brainy—tonight there's only Jeremy and me left, he thought with melancholy. They're all wearing contacts now. Everyone's pretty because everyone's for sale. It's time I switched to contacts.

He saw Maya, who was starting to show her forty years. Fred was giving her a yard of the old baloney: "You really could do any of those parts Julie and Rachel are doing. In fact, you could play the part of the French girl in A.C.'s film—"

"The film's finished, Fred. Haven't you heard?"

"Honey, I'm just saying that's the sort of part I'd like to see you do next."

"Yes, Fred, you're quite right," she said tartly.

A.C. remembered Fred saying only last week in his office, "Maya: no one wants to see her name—except buried in the pavement of Hollywood Boulevard—dead and forgotten—I tell ya."

A.C. shuddered. He walked over to a recessed window where Walt, the old-timer, was watching the slow progress of the house.

"Walt, how are you, buddy?"

"Fine, kiddo. This really is a funny feeling, isn't it? Watching the town go by from the window of your house?"

"Yeah, sure." A.C. wanted to change the subject; he wanted good news for a change.

"How are ya, Walt? Watcha preparing? A comedy?"

"Naw, a musical version of *Private Lives*. Rachel said she'll do it as soon as she sees the script and Larry's real interested."

Not such a bad idea, but, Jesus, why ask. He knew very well that whatever Walt was preparing wouldn't get off the ground. Walt was too old and his last films had lost money. So what got into him to ask?

"Yeah, great idea, wish I'd thought of that myself. –Excuse me, Walt, I must get something to drink. Can I get you something?"

"No, kiddo. I'm doing fine. Fabulous house, A.C., and a swell housewarming," and he added as if he knew that A.C.'s luck had changed, "Mildred and I are going now. We get up early–we go jogging every morning at seven."

A.C. made his way painfully through the crowd. He was looking for Kitty now. The little boy in him called from the depths of his childhood for the woman who would take him in her arms and rock away the sorrow. "Kitty–Kitty!"

He saw her blond hair from the back of the room and elbowed his way toward her. She was talking to a man called Zuckmann or Zuckermann, a new executive at MGM. Neat, trim, well pressed, and well brushed, he was the perfect lawyer-executive type. He was wearing his contacts all right–his eyes had that glint as he listened to Kitty, his head slightly to one side, lips parted in a faint smile. A furtive suspicion went through A.C.'s mind. No, no, not possible. Kitty is happy. I give her everything she could hope for.

"Kitty!" A.C. called above the noise.

She didn't turn around, just put up her hand in a gesture that meant for him not to interrupt because she was busy, and as he got closer he heard her say, "Sixteen rooms really–the three extra ones are just large closets–and eight bathrooms–all the original tiles–it was built in 1891 by a Chicago stockyard millionaire who retired here with his family. I'm getting antique wallpapers from England."

The exec was impressed, he put on a concerned expression.

"You're restoring an American heirloom—our cultural legacy," and he added shrewdly, "Are you getting the expenses off your taxes? You should, you know. There is a tax grant for that sort of thing—restoration of antiques. I could look into it, if you wanted me to."

A.C. didn't feel like talking to her anymore. The shaking of the house suddenly made him seasick. He needed fresh air. He made his way to the closest window, but it was jammed or nailed down. He hugged the wall and slid along it, looking for a door. There was a lot of noise, so many people laughing, having fun, doing this absurd, meaningless stomping on the beat, not even looking at each other, not touching either. Once in a while someone would leave the floor to make his way toward the bar and get a drink or some food and his partner would stay on, not even aware of the other's departure. A few people were drunk, girls mostly. Funny how it was often the girls who got drunk at parties, the men were too busy boasting about their projects—and when the women got drunk they complained about their husbands or their maids in repetitive, slurred speeches. Others were so stoned they were just off, unreachable.

At last he found a door. He pulled it open with such strength it almost stayed in his hand. Now he was on the moving platform, vacillating, all alone on the narrow ledge. Only a little jump and he would be free of the evil old house. He twisted his ankle as he fell to the ground, awkwardly, just by a magnolia tree. He sat there and hugged the dark trunk. It was solid and smelled slightly of ivy and moss. His eyes closed, he clung to the solid trunk while the bewitched old house quavered away under its load of dedicated revelers–swaying and sliding and thrusting and thumping–rock–thump–rock. No one missed him.

The Cat-o'-nine-tails

Dark. Dense darkness all around. The air smelled cold and antiseptic; it reminded her of that place where her tonsils had been removed. Where was she? She wasn't home, that she knew. She tried hard but she couldn't remember where she was. One thing called itself urgently to her attention; in fact, that was what had woken her up: she needed to pee-pee, badly, or disaster would strike. She heard a creaking of springs, a rustling of cloth, and something between a sigh and a whimper, like the yelps little dogs make during their sleep when they dream of being punished. Now that she listened carefully, she could also hear soft respirations. At last she was awake enough to remember. She was in the dormitory of a boarding school, her bed one of eight or ten; strangers were sleeping in the other beds, girls who belonged here and had indicated their territorial rights, made her feel insignificant, unwanted. Consciousness of the present brought back to her mind the painful moments of her arrival this morning, her father having driven along all those mountain curves, watchful of the precipice on her side of the road, which had caused her to be sick out of the window of the Citroën; her mother had hugged her for the rest of the voyage.

Desolation had gripped her when the big house had been revealed, massive and forbidding, ensconced on the side of the mountain, surrounded by dark pine trees. When the inevitable moment to part had come, her mother had cried, just as she had when the doctor had said that her little girl was too thin for her height and that tuberculosis was threatening her. Claire had been made to understand then, just as she had this morning, that the fault was hers, because of some stubborn determination to fast in the hope of bringing back the love and caring of the one person she could not do without, whom she hardly saw now, except at night after she had been put to bed by her nanny, since a mysterious drama had taken place in her mother's life, a rift, a fissure in her marriage, a disappointment so great that she had lost interest in her own child. Since that estrangement, the celestial apparition would drop in for a minute only on her way to her soirées, stand in the doorway of the dark bedroom, cut out in a halo of light as befitted her beauty, a zephyr of perfume emanating from her radiant fairness. Although Claire was but a child and could not have explained the intricate mechanism of her own comportment, she felt confusedly that she had now lost interest in her own existence, could fail to sustain it, forget to breathe now that her mother viewed her with distracted indifference. She knew that she had been banished from her mother's orbit and nothing could bring her back in.

Trying to find her bearings in the dark, not so much in order to learn her way in this establishment as not to fail her mother and disgrace herself publicly, she thought she could situate the window somewhere in front of her, and the door leading to the corridor where the bathroom was, in a straight line on her left. She climbed down from the high bed and started on her course across the large room. The tiles were cold and hard to her feet but she could not possibly look for her slippers; anyway, she had now recklessly left her berth and was engaged on the perilous voyage across the thick darkness. She placed her feet hesitatingly one in front of the other, such timid little steps that she had to extend her arms on each side to keep her balance, a little white form ghosting uncertainly through the black element, cold to breathe, infiltrating itself cold and hostile under her nightdress. She kept putting one toe in front of the other, going toward what she hoped was the direction of the door, hoping to have the right heading, but not sure now in this expanding vacuum.

This morning Mama had said to Colette, "You are older, so please look after Claire, won't you?" Colette had given her a sharp look and mumbled something with evident bad grace. Claire could see right through her to the core of her mangy little heart. She knew her to be as mean as her features were sharp. Why couldn't her mother see what was so obvious? Claire knew that from now on until the last day in that school she would have to suffer her cousin's tyranny or learn how to dodge her. And indeed, later, after her mother and father had departed, leaving her to face this new life as best she could, her cousin had used her senior prerogative to trail her around these vast classrooms permeated with the smell of ink and books, pretending to guide her and explain the rules: for instance, how in the mornings you had to submit to the burning pain of an ice-cold shower because it developed the character as well as a good circulation; only on Saturdays could you have a hot bath, and then again you might not be the first to lie in it; in fact, second- or third-year girls had priority and usually someone had peed in the water before you got in, besides leaving it slightly gray with soap and dirt and decidedly tepid. Colette lingered with particular relish on the punishment that awaited the wicked: for serious felonies, the cat-o'-nine-tails, each thong ending in a little ball of lead that cut deeply into your flesh and left ineffaceable scars. Colette herself had never seen the instrument of torture, but she knew that it existed, locked up in the headmistress's office. The legend of famous whippings that had left the offender bleeding and permanently stigmatized had been handed down in the mythology of the school; the memory of the thrashings and the proof that these stories were authentic, preserved and pointed out to newcomers in the carving of initials on the many layers of shiny cream paint coating the toilet walls, the toilet having served as a cell where the culprits were locked up before sentence could be executed; the number of strokes was duly recorded in uneven numbers according to the wickedness of the crime: three strokes for insolence or defiance or inobservance of the rules, five for a theft of food or money, nine for an attempted escape. All these details were spelled out by Colette with the authority of one who belongs to the establishment, respects its wisdom, and would be forced to report any violation.

Claire was now haunted by the recollection of these chronicles; the thought of the whip hadn't left her mind since this morning. Right now she hoped that being caught at night in the middle of the dormitory without your slippers on wasn't on the list of offenses. She dreaded to think of what would happen if she didn't reach the door at the end of the room. She kept going, aware that she had been walking for what seemed a long time; she ought to be near her destination; it couldn't be far off now.

Mama had said to Miss Engle, the headmistress, "Please see to it that she eats, she's so thin."

Miss Engle had answered with a sickly smile, "Everyone is always hungry here—the open air, you know. Besides," she had added firmly, "I'll sit her next to me in the dining hall and I'll see to it that she finishes her plate."

Dinner had been a torture: the noise in the great hall during the assault on the tables by all those grimacing children so free and boisterous had perturbed her, with the result that Claire had retreated into a painful muteness and had been totally unable to eat her dinner. Miss Engle kept looking at her from the corner of her eyes, watching every forkful with growing disapprobation.

Yet Mama had said, "Do everything Miss Engle tells you, my darling. Be a good girl." But how could she possibly eat those fried eggs, burned and rubbery on the bottom, fringed with curled brown edges and yet runny on the top, the yolk barely lukewarm? Her stomach had heaved several times; fortunately she had been able to control it, but the food could not be swallowed. Rubbery and dry, it had stayed in her left cheek, a passage left open to swallow the yogurt and canned peaches. She had gone to sleep with the food still in her mouth and fervently hoped that now was her chance to spit out the nauseating stuff into the toilet bowl. Surely Miss Engle would not find out if she did so in the middle of the night.

She crept on stealthily, trying not to bump into any objects, shoes, bed, or chair, but the walls had inexplicably receded with her every step. She could not understand why she had not reached her destination yet. Perhaps she had been distracted and had changed course without realizing it. She felt she was in a nebulous void, doomed to wander all night. She could not even hear the breathing of the other girls anymore. Had she without knowing it entered another room bigger and emptier still? Panic seized her, she tried several directions, and finally reached a wall, but although she kept sliding along it, she never came to any door. It was clear that the spiteful forces that governed the school and inhabited the bodies of Colette and Miss Engle had now maliciously blocked the door. To add to her misery, she was now unsure whether she would be able to control her bladder.

In order to alleviate the immense loneliness of her predicament, she emitted plaintive little sounds. If the door didn't exist anymore, if the beds had disappeared and all the girls with them, at least she was still alive, the sound of her voice confirmed it. Presently her whimpers reached her own heart, she felt that Claire, this little girl of four lost in the dark, was immensely pitiable; she deserved tears to flow for her, solidarity required that she should weep; why should she restrain herself when she was entirely alone in this hostile darkness? While she sobbed aloud, she admired inwardly her tones of distress; yes, she was convincing; she hoped against all hope that her mother would hear and rescue her, while at the same time she didn't care if she was heard by the governing body of this establishment, convinced as she was that its inhabitants had forsaken her. She sobbed violently.

Presently a ray of light appeared, cutting as if by magic the contour of a door on the wall opposite. Steps were heard, getting nearer; sleepy grunts, exclamations, and coiling of bedsprings brought back sounds of life around her, and finally the door was mysteriously found, opened, breaking the darkness in an oblong shape of yellow light spilling into the room, ending on the floor in the point of a triangle. In the diffused glow bleeding from the bright doorway, the dormitory reappeared, its rows of little beds miraculously back in their previous arrangement, several girls sitting up, bewildered with sleep, blinking like bats in the sunlight. Claire stood her ground, bawling with terror at the thought of the whip, waiting for the inevitable chastisement now that warm urine was running ignominiously down her legs.

She looked at the silhouette cut out in the doorway, tried to make out which hand held the dreaded cat-o'-nine-tails, while the shape came closer, closer, closer yet. Claire cried out when two hands grabbed her under the arms and a voice said softly, "Don't cry, child–don't be frightened–the bathroom is this way."

Stardom, at Last

"How're you feeling this morning, honey?"

"Gross! Can't wait for this thing to come out."

"What thing, honey?"

"This baby. What do you think I mean?"

"What baby? Where? Are you pregnant?"

"Affirmative. I'm seven months gone."

"Jesus, honey! Who says so?"

"My gyno. Can't you see?"

"No, I can't. You just look a little plump, that's all. Where do you keep it?"

"Well, I'm careful about my diet."

"I'll say you are! But what about the film, sweetheart?"

"My part only starts in two months. It will be over by then."

"Won't you be tired? You should rest about two months after a baby. Well, one month maybe, if you're not breast-feeding."

"Breast-feeding, hell no!" exclaims Eve, and she sings:

"Rough winds do shake the darling buds of May,
And summer's lease hath all too short a date."

Never mind the darling buds, thinks Gertie, I must get her ready for the test. She unwinds the rollers from the luxuriant flaming hair, emblem of Eve Gordon's individuality, a plentiful halo which she so likes to toss in defiance of the mundane, of the insipid banality of life that would be her lot had she remained Thelma Gordon, the little girl who set her eyes so firmly on the tarnished screen of her local drive-in.

"You sure look pale, honey. Do you eat properly?" Gertie asks to keep things pleasant.

"I prefer it that way. I hate the sun. Oh, the vulgarity of the California look! My dear, Garbo never had a tan."

And Eve checks in the mirror her Pre-Raphaelite paleness, admires her wondrous black eyes carboned around to achieve a soulful if slightly haunted look.

A knock on the door and the first assistant, always the bearer of bad news, comes in.

"Yes, Jerry. I'd love a bottle of champagne and a rose-petal salad. How kind of you to ask."

Eve thinks: You never catch Jerry Morton smiling, not unless the director cracks a joke. She can sense venomous glee, though well concealed behind his baby blue eyes.

"Miss Gordon, I called your agent this morning to tell him that we've had to reschedule and your part is now at the start of the film, that's in one week, with the location in two months' time, as planned."

"Oh no! You can't do that to me!"

"I'm very sorry. There is no other way," he moans comprehensively; "we lose your sets in four weeks. The studio has signed away the space for the Tim McCloud film. Is there any problem? Your agent said it was all right."

"No, it's not all right. Don't they have any respect? Their property, that's what I am, no more than a chair–"

"I'm sorry, Miss Gordon. I don't want to be indiscreet, but I think it's good for you to be spread out over the whole schedule–you know, for the press; of course, they'll have to recast you if you are not free."

"I'm not ready, I haven't studied the part yet."

"You have a week, isn't–"

"No it isn't. Don't you know that a serious actress needs a month to prepare? I have to learn to think as Carla, walk as Carla, breathe as Carla. How do you expect me to do all this in a week?"

Another winning smile spreads on Jerry's innocent face.

"I've come to tell you, Miss Gordon, because the press will be on the set during your tests, and I thought you might want to have the dates right. They're expecting you in half an hour."

"Thanks so much for the good news, Jerry," she hisses. "Oh, I won't be able to face them! Why didn't they tell me sooner?"

He makes a sorry-about-that grimace. And he repeats as if to an idiot child, "I'll send you the car right here, at hairdressing, in half an hour, to take you on the set. Thank you, Miss Gordon."

The concerned tilt of the head, his hand already gripping the doorknob: "Can I send anything from the commissary? Anything you'd like? Though I don't think champagne . . . before a film test . . . the press . . . Coffee perhaps, and a sandwich?"

"No thanks, Jerry, you've done enough for one day."

The door discreetly shut, there is a long silence while Gertie stuffs pins in her mouth so she won't have to speak first. As long as she's been on the studio payroll she has managed to keep out of trouble. She thinks: Watch out girl, there are no other films starting right now, if Eve gets sore at you you'll be put on suspension just when you and Harry are about to move to a new house.

Eve explodes. "Gertie, please, Gertie, brush out that wedding cake. You know I want to look natural. You've piled curls on Elizabeth Taylor too long. Please get rid of that silicone look!"

"Calm yourself, hon. Haven't brushed out the setting yet. Here, put your head down. Elizabeth Taylor never did have such gorgeous hair anyway."

Eve tries to think about her role in this new movie. At last it had happened, just the part to allow her to prove to all her vulnerability, the transparent crystal of her soul, the swift changes of emotions she is so capable of. And she thinks with anguish about that small heart beating inside her, stealing, she feels, her precious chance at fame, the freedom she cherishes, claiming her attention which belongs rightfully to films, literature, or vaster political engagements. "It has a right to live, yes, but should let me fulfill my own destiny." She chases the disturbing thought away. "Later, I'll make a decision later."

"Honey," says Gertie with earnest conviction, "if you want my opinion you're not pregnant at all. Probably a crooked gyno who wants your visits at sixty bucks a go. Then one day he'll tell you it was a nervous pregnancy or something." And she adds authoritatively, "As far as I am concerned you haven't even got a doughnut in that belly of yours."

So at one-thirty Eve Gordon enters Stage 16. Head

high, challenging the ghosts of Rita and Marilyn and Elizabeth, and before them the Divine One, trying not to be affected by the cavernous expanse of cement, the smell of sawed wood and paint and the particular acridity of carbon that lingers after the great arc lights have been switched off. (How many times has she longed for the cry "Kill the brutes," for the end of the ordeal, the relief that follows the snapping one by one of the switches!)

This time she enters the set in style. Her name will be above the titles glaring and shimmering, same size as Stanford Ames's, so she has her retinue: her hairdresser, makeup man, wardrobe woman, and June, the stern and massive Cherokee woman in charge of body makeup, her only true friend among these others, studio informers all.

She knows it is essential to hide from the press and crew the panic that seizes her each time she enters a set. "Hiya, Joe!" she shouts to the cameraman. "How are you, you lean so and so?" Without waiting for the answer, she rushes off. "Oh, Jack, my love, isn't it going to be great!" —in the arms of the director. Kiss on the mouth, pat on the back, superlatives straight from the heart. The press is gratified.

"The new star. Hollywood's new discovery. They're putting everything they've got into her," drones the press guy.

"Once again, Eve, give us that kiss again!"

Delightful and girlish in her ample black skirt tightly belted at the waist, Eve throws her head back, tosses her hair into position, gushes with that throaty laugh, and kisses the old mouth she met only once at a party. The press asks her to comment, illuminate, define, and qualify for the benefit of all her fans:

"Oh, yes, thrilled, of course Jack Armintage—my favorite director—I start in a week. I play throughout the movie —such a thrilling lady, Carla, tender and vulnerable—no, never before with Jack or Stanford Ames, this is my first time. Eve is just born, you might say. Why so? Because Jack loves women, you can see that plainly in all his films. Well, he can find a soul in a cement block, fish out femininity in an Olympic swimmer. The Nobel of filmmakers —what more can I say, gentlemen? I trust him. Right, Jack? I trust you—Eve will bite the old apple any day for you, Jack."

"A winner! A legitimate actress! The new star!"

The press pop away their flashes, forgetting that last week or last year they said the same stuff about what's-her-face.

So now Jack gives the signal for the test to start. Eve presents her coquettish eye to her Cyclops lover, the camera. A toss of the luxuriant mane, a languid turn to the right, a sultry pucker of the mouth, that smile again, not to forget genuine innocence and real Simon-pure fervor.

Gray-haired, dressed in his elegant overalls, Jack approves, mildly enthusiastic, his memory frozen on his illustrious past, his mind fixed on the ninth hole he will putt in tomorrow.

"Magic, angel, real magic," Jack purrs on. "Now turn to the right. Fine. Now give us the left one. Gentlemen, I give you the most beautiful profile that ever hit the screen."

Early evening. Crumpled in her left hand, a torn piece of paper with a barely legible address scribbled on it. Eve drives nervously, looking for Formosa Avenue. Her heart beats wildly. What will she tell him that he can understand? "Doctor, I feel so sick, I haven't eaten a real meal in three weeks"? He won't believe it. Or this: "Depression. Yes, despair so overpowering, I fear I might kill myself"? Could he understand the real motivation? The drive, the urge to play Carla, tender moving Carla, the definite woman? Her mind then wanders back to today's encounter with the camera and her eyes fill with tears of frustration. "My cheeks are too plump. Did I use enough shading? Oh, God, I didn't show Jack I can cry just like that in front of the camera. I'll call him later."

Eve is ushered into the fake-leather and pressed-wood sanctuary, where misty photographs advertise the tenderness of motherhood. Across the desk, Dr. Sullivan approves, encourages benignly. Eve realizes at once that she doesn't have to give reasons. The doctor seems eager to believe her story about being two weeks overdue and uncomfortable beyond bearing. She is amazed at the flow of reassuring banalities among which she registers a few pointed questions.

"Your husband agrees? No husband, well, that's life. They come and go, don't they? And your parents, no religious reservations? They don't know, all the better, it'll be a nice surprise."

In a smooth voice, he murmurs, "Eight hundred in cash. Don't eat or drink past midnight, not even water. Tomorrow morning at seven, I'll come to your place and give you an injection; a second one, a third one if need be. We'll wait until the contractions are every thirty seconds, perhaps until the waters break; then we'll call an ambulance. Someone else will deliver you, a colleague of mine. You can trust him."

Her heart beats incoherently, she'd like to ask him the

burning question. But if she dared say, "Doctor, will he live?" he would answer, would he not, "But of course, the little fellow is overdue; why ask?"

Cocooned in whiteness, silence, and shiny metal, Eve wakes up with instant consciousness. She has only been out a few seconds, it seems. "Oh, God, it hasn't been done yet!" Touching her swollen belly, she rings for the nurse.

"What happened? Why isn't it born yet?"

"He is born. It's a boy."

"How nice. Can I see it?"

"Impossible, hon. He's in the incubator. He's lucky to be alive. Two pounds one ounce only."

Unconcerned, Eve murmurs wearily, "Yeah, slimness runs in the family. Nurse, I am famished, can I have a smoked salmon sandwich on whole wheat, please."

"No, hon, you'd be sick. You must rest now. In an hour or so I'll bring you some tea."

Eve's head sinks back on the pillow. Shutting her eyes, her mind floats hazily on this new conjuncture, this permutation in the order of things. Is she happy? She can't answer. But she knows one thing, she is grateful that this thing is out and alive. She also knows that part of her flesh has been chipped off. From now to the end of her life, she must reckon with this duplication, conjugate in the plural. Oh, the hassle of it!

A day later, supported by the nurse, her entrails falling to the floor, or so it feels, Eve stands in front of the glass partition where she can see the incubator. Presented in its plastic bubble, as if it were a jewel, the grimacing little chit of life moves feebly in pain and protest. Eve reflects with distaste that she could never bear the sight of monkeys at the zoo; now this wrinkled thing is a worse eyesore yet. How can this be her baby?

"Are you sure it's mine?" she insists, almost hoping she'll be told hers is no more.

"Sure, hon. We mark them at birth, right in the operating room."

"The poor thing!"

She feels defeated, deeply injured. Why should she, after careful retracing of her past, correcting of circumstances, all in the pursuit of harmony and beauty, be inflicted with this shriveled little runt? Mistaking her feelings, the nurse comforts her.

"Don't worry, hon. He'll start gaining weight soon. He's doing fine, fighting hard. What will you call him? Have you got a name yet?"

"I don't know. I haven't thought. 'Baby' for now."

"You'll have to register him this afternoon. Think of a name, hon. I'll give you a list," says the nurse encouragingly.

"I feel so tired," says Eve.

Back in her bed, exhausted, Eve massages lanolin into her stomach in an effort to erase the lines already grooved in her belly by this fetus, the perverted vision she cannot chase away printed indelibly on her mind. Her heart aches and she cries with frustration for this living thing sparked off in an embrace with a man who threw her off long since, because he had sensed her designs on him. Conceived through calculated coupling and grown in her womb with the food she ate, not for this child but for herself, not in view to give him strength but to nourish her own beauty. "Oh, God, why this joke on me?" And while she rubs in the cream, Eve sings to herself the lullaby her mother would hum to her when she was a girl and her stomach cried with a hunger so pressing that she could not go to sleep.

Dawn is particularly undramatic in Beverly Hills. A blanching of darkness heralded by the starting up of innumerable cars precedes the eight o'clock pall of opaqueness, wherein all colors blend in a diffusion of gray, and only close by can you see the palm tree fighting for its splash of green.

Risen from her hospital bed, Eve slides into her car, keyed up because so fearful of today's challenge. The morning almost a continuation of yesterday, as the night was but a fretful mobilization of all her ammunition. Today, on her first day of filming, Eve Gordon meets Stanford Ames, easily the highest-paid star in the industry. Today Eve Gordon is a star. Everything coincides to prove it: the respectful greetings of the crew, the complicity of the cameraman, the size of her dressing room, her chair with her name printed on the back. (Where do they go, these printed panels, after the film is finished and the star of today falls into oblivion? Are they shredded like the President's memos, burned on the back lot, or used to consolidate the plaster decor of a Mexican village, or are they piously stored in the garage of a fetishist fan?) Eve wishes she could enjoy her moment of triumph, only she feels so weak and worn.

And so the day starts on its endlessly repeated mosaic of small gestures. Sprawled in his chair next to the camera, Jack Armintage studies her, wondering: What's the matter with her? She's got no life, even her voice is drab. Aloud, he articulates the instructions he first gave to that blonde, what's-her-name, still serviceable advice after thirty years.

"Give me more energy, angel, that's what the camera picks up, energy. I want to feel energy behind those lovely black eyes! Once again, kiddos. Silence, please!"

Eve would give anything to lie right there on the floor, sleep, and forget. But not yet. She repeats inwardly her magic incantation, "The camera is my lover, my caressing tender lover," going through the scene for the umpteenth time, hoping that the probing eye will pick up the gift of self in the moist parting of her lips.

"Real, Eve, make it real! Inside you, angel, not on your face. The camera wants to see your guts, remember. Once again. Silence, please!"

Once again, and once again, and again. Jack is now bored and mumbles, sulking, "Print take two."

During lunch with her partner, Eve wishes she could unburden her heart. She feels a misery more biting than salt on an open wound. She can only ask Stanford, "What's the matter? Is it him or me?"

"Whiskey-sodden old bastard. He's got a zona; takes it out on you."

Soothingly, Stanford offers encouragement, a glass of wine, and protection, all gratefully accepted. Without effort he assumes, off the set, the part written for him in the script, and Eve gives the right cue.

They come back to the sound stage united in this new alliance. Once again, Eve feels the winner when Stanford gives her a nod or a smile. Jack, that old lion, is wise to the game. Nothing could be healthier for the film than the two stars plotting their scenes together. Good kids, now I may get a performance out of her, he hopes. And the cast and crew start again with the patience of children building a sand castle, resigned, content with its ephemeral life.

At six o'clock, to everyone's relief, the shout "It's a

wrap!" rings across the set. The decor immediately plunged into dusty death after the lights snap off one by one, the shadows of night brushing past the make-believers of day. Eve, off balance for a moment, wakes from her dream to resume the self left in suspension since slipping on her costume, long ago this morning.

Driving her car on the way home, Eve with a mixture of hope and misgiving recapitulates today's work. From time to time her mind drifts back with pleasure to the thought of Stanford: his way of leaning forward slightly, head tilted, hand fanned open on the hip, while watching her. All in all, today had a color and shape that smile at Eve Gordon. Only a small, buzzing, undefined thought nags her. Oh yes, now she remembers: that disturbing object, ugly as refuse, left to survive in its plastic bubble, somewhere on the fourth floor of the hospital.

Eve's car swerves off the slow trail, purring obediently up the canyon as if still on the assembly line. She reaches the hospital just in time to see through the glass partition the nurse, hooded in white cap and mouthpiece, change and clean with infinite care, so as not to chafe the vulnerable skin or injure the jellied bones, her stunted infant. The needle is still planted in the fontanel, feeding endlessly the drops of life-giving fluid. As the nurse comes out, Eve grabs her arm.

"Has he gained weight yet? He seems so puny still."

"I don't know, hon. I'm not here in the mornings when they weigh them. Look at the chart."

"Two ounces only. He's only gained two ounces in five days."

"They lose weight the first three days, hon."

"Does he cry often?"

"I wouldn't know. We've got six more in the ward. We

haven't got time to see which one is crying. But it's a good sign when they do. Means they're getting stronger."

And as the nurse waddles away, smacking off her rubber gloves, a seed of pity germinates in Eve's heart for this miniature of herself in which she can recognize the hungry gesture for survival.

The next day gallops forward with the trepidation of Eve's heartbeat. Colorado Jim, propman and set dresser, "Running Jim," as Stanford Ames calls him, stretches out crisp new sheets for the bed scene. A forest of spotlights, standing in the same random disorder as television antennas on a Roman roof, project their angles of light on the two stars. Eve feels vulnerable. Molded in her T-shirt, she feels exposed, her swollen breasts revealed to prying eyes. She cuddles in Stanford's arms looking for comfort while Carla, tender vulnerable Carla, expresses her anguish.

"Jonathan, I feel you're going away from me. Don't you trust me?" As he looks for his cigarettes she talks on, pleading for the right to be listened to.

"Last night I dreamed that my brother and I were children again. We were in a forest. He was ahead of me, walking faster and faster, and I started to run after him, crying, 'Please wait for me, don't leave me behind.'" She stops for a second while Stanford-Jonathan turns the sound up on the stereo. "Are you listening to me, or just listening to that record?"

And Stanford-Jonathan answers impassively, "Why do you go back to him every night? And I don't mean your brother. Hand me that ashtray, will you?"

Eve stretches her arm in a gesture programmed during rehearsals, but then stops in mid-air. She has discovered, seen the spots. First one spot and then the other, definitely darker, revealing her nipples where the damp cloth is now transparent. Her hand stopped in mid-air, her mouth caught open with surprise, no words coming out, forgetting the lines, even forgetting to breathe for a few seconds, her eyes darting fearfully. Has anyone noticed? Has Stanford? Has Jack? She springs out of bed without a word and while Stanford watches her, aroused sexually by her distress as well as by the dampness of her breasts, Eve runs for June, urging, pleading, whispering.

"June, help me! Do something—look, I've spotted my T-shirt."

And June, surprised: "Honey, what's happening to you? Is that milk? Why do you have milk?"

And Eve, imperative: "Don't ask, for heaven's sake! Just dry me and stop it flowing."

And now Jack thunders over the confusion.

"What is it? What's wrong? Jerry, see what's wrong with Eve. Come on now, we've got to finish this scene. Let's go!"

After a while, in the secrecy of her portable dressing room, with the electric hair dryer covering the whispering and then June rushing out for adhesive tape, slamming the door after her, and Jerry Morton knocking several times to no avail, and finally explaining to Jack that there must be something wrong with her hair, Eve finally emerges from the trailer, a crisp smile fixed on her face. Sensing the quivering distress behind that smile, but cautious as men will be for whom women's bodies and minds are a mysterious territory, Jack perceives that something of momentous significance has taken place. Why else would her acting now be so erratic? She stumbles on the same words, always at that same spot where she reaches for the ashtray, until Jack finally breaks out impatiently.

"Listen, sweetheart, if you're not comfortable with that line, speak in your own words, but say something."

Eve smiles thinly and starts again, awkward words coming out of her mouth, now trailing into a fit of nervous laughter, which painfully ends in tears. Resigned, Jack knows that he won't have that master shot.

"Relax, angel, we'll break it up into small fragments. Let's start on Stanford. Have a rest. Drink a cup of coffee."

Stanford whispers warmly, "Let's have dinner tonight, you and I. Right?"

The dinner had been a good one. Japanese sashimi, sukiyaki, and all that. Stanford had been nice. True, he looked a little bored as he listened to the story of her childhood on the farm, but she had been smart enough to keep it short. She had laughed when he had said, "Skip to the punch line, will you." Thank God, she was sharp when it came to wisecracking. Later, she had done her Isadora stunt, long glittering scarf floating through the car window, reciting Byron with a French accent, though she knew just as well as anyone else that Isadora was American, and besides she was a dancer, not an actress. Never mind, the air smelled of tuberose and Eve had been moved to recite:

> "She walks in beauty, like the night
> Of cloudless climes and starry skies."

That was when he had grabbed her by the neck, pulled her face close to his, and after parking the Rolls with the smoothest swoop, kissed her nice and slow while she was still laughing. And now he was driving to her place, one cunning hand exploring under her silk jersey dress, moving up her stockinged flesh, while the other was on the wheel.

Outside her bedroom, the buddleia knocks its gentle bough, Eve wonders, "When did Eloise change the sheets? Oh yes, when I was in the . . ." Eve prefers not to finish the thought, not to remember that what is about to happen is in reckless defiance of the doctor's orders. She crawls luxuriantly naked between the cream sheets, her breasts dry now, thank goodness, and less painful too. She listened to the tap in the bathroom, down the corridor, gurgling as usual when opened fully. Her mind floating from the splash of water to the clatter of applause and the sweetest dream coming within reach, almost palpable: Stanford Ames, in love with her, deferentially opening the door of a limo, while fans chant their names in cadence and cameramen flash away tender close-ups.

But suddenly Stanford is there beside her, overpowering her, his minty-fresh mouth greedily claiming hers. She surrenders to the emotion, lulled and soothed with well-being, moaning with each sweet surprise, soon unable to name which portion of her is being aroused as each secret part vibrates toward an unbearable pitch. But suddenly, without warning . . . Why? Why has he stopped? What happened? What did he feel? The violent suspension of motion jars her. A few seconds filled with silent horror, then abruptly he rips back the sheet, smacking the cloth in anger, to reveal, uncover—"Oh no, no!"—the dark red flow, viscous as saliva, gumming his genitals, now spreading on the sheets. She gasps while he jumps out of bed, rushes to the bathroom to grab two towels, one for himself, the other thrown at her. And still the sticky sweet warm blood oozing out of her, leaving her faint and nauseous.

"What is this?" he yells. "What's happening to you? Should I call a doctor? Don't move, for God's sake!"

She cries out of her heart, ashamed, frightened.

"I'm sorry, Stanford. Oh, God, make it stop! Give me some brandy, please—in the living room—it's not true, that little brat won't leave me alone."

After he called the doctor, and while they are waiting for him to come, she tells all: she tells about the child she kept until too late, because she thought this man, her lover, would leave his wife for her. But he was very firm, said he wouldn't leave his children, even to have one with her. He had left her plenty of money to have the child when it became clear there was no other way but to have it.

"But when? I never even heard you were pregnant."

"Six days ago. That's why I'm so tired, I guess."

"Ah yes. I saw your breasts were giving milk today on the set."

"You noticed?"

"Yeah, I noticed."

Stanford is trying hard to understand. His mind is clouded. There are questions he doesn't really want to ask.

"You were pregnant when you did the tests ten days ago?"

"Sure I was pregnant."

That black skirt, tight at the waist, he remembers it. No, he hadn't noticed anything then. It didn't show, didn't show at all.

"He must have been so small. Did you have a miscarriage?"

"Well . . . he was seven months already. They're formed at seven months."

"Is he alive?"

She nods.

"He's fine. He'll be all right, I'm sure."

He looks her in the eyes, the question exploding in him with such violence he wonders why she does not hear it. The question remains unasked, humming between them like electric wires taut between two poles. Her answer at last, as clearly defined as if she had said, "Yes, it was. It was induced," but she does not say that. Instead she says, "Listen, Stan, this is the best part I've ever been offered. Do you understand?"

"Sure, sweetheart. Sure, sure, I understand."

He must go now, can't wait any longer, puts his clothes on in a hurry, hoping the doctor will come soon. When he finally arrives, Eve asks Stanford softly, "Please don't tell Jack or anyone else. Okay? Promise me you won't?"

"Sure, you can count on me. Good night, sweetheart. Have a good rest now."

A little reluctantly, he adds, "Call me if you need anything. Here's my private number. The other one is the answering service."

The next morning, Stanford is called early by Jerry Morton.

"Mr. Ames, I'm sorry, but we have a change in the schedule. Miss Gordon is sick and we'll do the scenes in your office. We'll start rehearsing at nine. Thank you, Mr. Ames."

When Stanford comes on the set, he finds Jack slumped in his chair, puffing on his pipe, seemingly in profound contemplation of a lamp. As usual, his cup of coffee is getting cold. Startled out of his reverie, he points a finger.

"Pull up a chair, Stan. I want to talk to you."

Stanford notices the spot under his lips where he has forgotten to shave, a sure sign of upset.

"I tried to call you last night, only you were out. The

thing is this: I'll be frank with you, I haven't been pleased with the rushes."

He touches Stanford on the arm, affectionately.

"Not you. I mean Eve. She's got some kind of block and I can't break it down. She gives out something hard and artificial. I don't know how else to tell you. This film depends on the public believing her, see. By the way, she's sick today. Jerry must have told you, right? And that's another thing—she looks bad. Maybe she lost a lot of weight or something. . . . I need your help, Stan. The studio wants to fire her—I told them, come on, give her another chance."

Stanford feels uneasy. He has spent a bad night. After coming home, he had poured himself a whiskey, something he doesn't believe in. But hell, he could still feel the slippery warm blood all over him, and the patch spreading on the sheets. He had taken a long shower. Then he had watched a film on "The Late Show." He couldn't even remember what it was. At about three in the morning he had finally dropped off to sleep.

"The kid's had some trouble, Jack. She's going through bad times."

"She told you?"

"Yeah. I saw her last night. I'm sure she'll be all right after two or three days in bed. I know the part means a lot to her."

"Yeah, that's what I think, too. Thanks a lot, Stanford. We'll take it slowly. And listen, it's no sweat if you don't know the lines. Nobody expects you to be word perfect."

Six royal tuberoses, a gift from Stanford, stuck in a plastic waste paper basket, the open window drawing outside the waves of sweetness, too fragrant, almost putrescent.

But Eve doesn't look at the flowers. From her bed she watches a large black fly trying to get through the wire-mesh screen and enter her room. The insect's perseverance worries her, as if some insidious evil were determined to attack and soil her person. Her eyes, slit half-closed, follow the insect's efforts and she waits. Time seemingly stagnant, but soundlessly expanding into midday bloom, as the waxy tuberose buds will do before their decline. She waits for her strength to come back. Right now, just turning over in bed demands a gathering of all her energies. Her jar of honey next to her, there's a start. She takes a spoonful and watches the obstinate fly moving its legs and wings with a will to pierce the screen, and buzzing, buzzing.

The smell of tuberose reminds her of somewhere else, other times, way back when . . . She checks her padding. The blood seems to have stopped. Yes, she remembers the high bed in that other house. How was it situated? Sideways to the window, that's right. The small farm window, never really opened, never closed, just jammed forever; a slit large enough to let the flies in on hot summer days. Her mother, sinking into the lumpy mattress, almost touching the floor, the pail of bloodied towels beside the bed, too tired to go downstairs and empty it each time, and yet not wanting the children to do it for her. The smell of blood and urine permeating the room, and that wet bundle, her just-born brother, never leaving her mother's side. Little Thelma, as she was then, had hated the sight of blood ever since. Even her own menstruation was an offense, a tarring, a branding unreasonably inflicted upon her, a punishment for belonging to the poor.

The phone rings, chasing the shadows away.

"Hello?"

"Miss Eve Gordon?"

"Speaking."

"This is the D. Hospital. Dr. Chapman wants to speak to you."

"Yes?" she says, knotted immediately at the pit of her stomach.

"Miss Gordon? Dr. Chapman. Could you come over? I'd like to talk to you."

"I can't, Doctor. I'm unwell. I can't leave my bed. What is it?"

"I hate to say this over the phone. . . ." His voice hums imperturbably, now that he has decided to speak. "Your baby has developed pneumonia. You see, Miss Gordon, it's quite frequent after a premature birth."

A long silence while she wonders what she is supposed to feel; irritation seems to be her only reaction. She hears the usual reassuring words about intensive care and doing all that can be done. She interrupts dryly: "Does he have a chance?"

"It's hard to tell, Miss Gordon. Fifty-fifty, I'd say. Come if you can."

"Soon as I'm better. Thank you for calling, Doctor."

Her voice becoming suddenly weak: "Please call me if there is any change, will you, please?"

"You can be assured we will. Good-bye, Miss Gordon."

Abruptly the phone emits that aggravating metallic tone, vexing her unreasonably. She had forgotten about the baby, it is true. "Maybe that's why he became ill." She can visualize the little thing wheezing and trembling with fever, too weak to scream the unformed urge to return to the dark warmth of her womb. "Soon as I can, I'll go see him. Soon as I can," she promises herself.

Two days later she is back at work, with the doctor's permission. She is greeted by the crew with smiles and hugs and "Welcome back, honey!" But she knows that the ever-vigilant eye of the studio watches her, in the person of Jerry Morton, that is. In Jack she senses a reserve, a caution, a half-measure somewhere. She almost feels that a ring is drawn around her, isolating her, excluding her from the true epicenter of things. She sits alone in her movie-queen chair, her script on her lap, reading lines that don't echo in her mind, wondering in fact if Stanford is avoiding her.

"Why, Stan, come and sit with me and tell me if the motor of your Rolls is still tuned fine and sharp." But she senses that she treads on forbidden ground there. Quickly she adds, "How has the work gone since I left?"

Shifting from one foot to the other, Stanford stands there, his right shoulder already turned in the direction of departure.

"Just fine. We've done about twelve minutes. All good, I think. But it's been heavy on my own. Glad to have you back. Excuse me, sweetheart, I must go and change. We are redoing the bed scene next." And he walks off, indifferent, disengaged.

Eve turns her face away, mumbling some inaudible curse. And before she can ask, "Who said so?" or warrant to herself, "I'll get Jerry for that, the son of a bitch," Jack comes over and grabs both her hands.

"Eve darling," says he with honeyed charm, "I don't have enough coverage on the bedroom scene. What do you say we do it again? Do you feel up to it now? Are you rested enough? Think you could? You look very pretty today."

"Yes, of course, Jack." And she thinks: yeah, finesse with me and I'll show you. "Sure I'll do it, only it'll take me an hour or so," she says, "to look over the script. You see, Jack darling, I wasn't told this was on the schedule."

"It wasn't. We've only just decided. We were going on with two-oh-five, as planned, when Joe said he'd left half the lamps in place; he said he can reset in a jiffy."

Eve smiles sweetly.

"I'll try and be as quick as I can."

Now it's Jerry's turn to drop by. Unflappable, cravatted as tight as with a hangman's noose, navy-blue tie on a navy-blue shirt, flash as silk but not real silk—why is she reminded of that bluebottle trying to invade her bedroom the other day?

"Miss Gordon, we're redoing the bedroom scene next. Could you get ready, please."

"When was that written on the schedule, Jerry old boy?" Her voice quivering with anger but still in control.

"Oh, it was always on the schedule for your return. But you seemed to have trouble with that scene, so I didn't want to worry you by putting it on the call sheet," says Jerry with his ever-coy smile. "The stuff we shot is just no good. That's what the studio execs said. Anyway, there isn't enough coverage."

Eve looks at him with sudden intuition; for the first time she notices the elbows too faithful to the trunk, the slight knock-knees, the fallen arches, suggesting a childhood lingering beyond nature's reason.

"Jerry, you're as sweet as a bunch of roses, if you see what I mean. Listen, smiles, as I've just explained to Jack, it'll take me an hour to go through the lines again, seeing as you didn't let me in on the big secret." She walks away tall and imperious as any queen.

The door of her portable slammed shut, Eve cries out in anguish, "Oh, June, help me! I feel so nervous. I don't understand what's with Jack and Stanford and the rest of them. They're holding things back from me. What's going on?"

And while the hammers knock away somewhere on the other side of the stage, and the cameraman calls for the brutes to be lit up, naming each one by its number, the number called out by the first electrician to the men up there on the catwalks. June massages Eve's shoulders with expert hands, explaining with the old wisdom of her kind, "It's nothing, honey. It's normal that you should feel out of things. You've been gone three days and they've worked close together three days. Now that you're back on the set, you'll be number one again in no time."

The stage is set again, new sheets stretched on the bed by Colorado Jim, the bedside table dusted with rough hands used to leather and wood rather than a rag duster, all objects put back in place according to the Polaroid stills; with words already used up, emotions, surprises, and delights already spent, Eve and Stanford begin to rehearse again.

"Jonathan, I feel you're going away from me. Don't you trust me?" Jonathan reaches for his cigarettes while Carla goes on.

"Last night I dreamed that my brother and I were children again. We were in a forest. He was ahead of me, walking faster and faster, and I started to run after him, crying, 'Pete, oh, Pete, please w . . .' "

Way back in the dark regions of the stage, near the padded double door, the phone rings. Jack Armintage thinks: I bet Kovacs wants to come on the set to check on Eve. Can't he leave me alone, damn it?

"Are you listening to me, Jonathan, or just listening to that record?"

"Why do you go back to him every night? And I don't mean your brother. Hand me that ashtray, will you?"

The phone; the phone ringing still, frail but persistent.

"Goddammit, Jerry. Can't you answer that phone?"

No one expected this outburst. Every gesture suspended, all eyes turn on Eve, still with stupefaction.

Jack finally breaks up the long, shocked silence that ensues.

"What is it, angel? What's bothering you? You want me to put the red on? Would that help you concentrate?"

"It's all right. I'm sorry. Let's continue," says Eve. "Where do we take it from?"

Jerry's voice, resonant with grit and malice, shouts, "Telephone for Miss Gordon! The D. Hospital."

Jack, resigned, turns to Eve. "Do you want to hurry up and take it?"

For a moment Eve hesitates, weighing, calculating the possibilities. "No, Jack." And shouting back to Jerry: "Tell them I'm busy. Could they call back in half an hour? Or . . . no, tell them I'll call back soon as I'm free."

She can feel Stanford's eyes on her, even though she keeps hers down. Buddy, I don't need bad news now, and good news don't need me.

Aloud she says, "Where did you say, Jack?"

Two grips discreetly playing chemmy, matching the numbers on their dollars, distract Jack's concentration till he explodes.

"Just a minute. Listen, fellows, this scene is difficult enough without a whole lot of noise and futzing around. If you're not working, go get yourself a cup of coffee. Right!" And with a softer, almost caressing voice, "Let's go now–Stanford?"

"Hand me that ashtray, will you?"

"Oh yeah," Carla says, reaching for the object. She goes on, bitterness giving a metallic tone to her voice, "You do it on purpose, don't you? We've discussed this till the cows come home. You don't want to take me on and you accuse me of staying with Warren. What do you want out of me?"

"Stop crabbing, will you!" says Jonathan sweetly, almost tenderly. "I told you: pull out of that dumb marriage, live on your own, take a job. Might hurt at first, but do yourself a favor."

"If I get out of the house, he won't give me an allowance."

"Fuck the allowance! I'll help you get a job, I'll—"

Eve interrupts him almost brutally: "Listen, Jack, I feel that Jonathan should take me in his arms here. It's a big move he's asking of Carla. I've got to feel he's doing it out of love—that he will help her. As it is, it plays: 'Get yourself squared up and maybe I'll jog along with you in the mornings.' But that's not it. He should be with me all the way. Don't you agree?"

In the silence just long enough for a breath, the silence before Jack can answer, the phone emits again its frail but persistent tingle. This time Jerry's voice trumpets immediately, with as little tact as possible: "For Miss Gordon! It's the D. Hospital again. They insist."

Eve goes to the phone, walking evenly, to meet what can no longer be avoided.

Left alone beneath the lights, who will speak first, Jack or Stanford? At last Jack brings the cold cup of coffee to his lips, the motion prelude to his speaking.

"Stan, I don't know what to do anymore. Nothing's coming out of her and she thinks it's your fault. I know, I know . . ."

Stanford looks at him silently, then shakes his head with a sigh.

"What do you say, Stan, you've got to act with her? I can see you're affected. You can't even take her in your arms and I know why. She's hard. What do you say?"

Stanford thinks for a second while the vision of three nights ago unravels in his mind. In a low, defeated voice he says, "No, I can't act with her. I can't even look her in the eyes." Staring at Jack, he asks quietly, "What does the studio say? And Kovacs—what does he want?"

Jack answers flatly, "They're ready to give her the ax. Kovacs, too—he wants her out."

Stanford looks dreamily at the cement between his feet. He nods his head once or twice.

"Yeah, yeah," he assents softly.

Eve comes back, trying to stifle the words that reverberate in her ears: "Your baby didn't pull through, Miss Gordon. He died this morning at 10:33. I'm so sorry."

"I mustn't think about it now, she repeats to herself. "I must get on with my work."

Weekend

At last he was here. At long last. She was worn out with the torment of waiting. She opened the door, her face transfixed with joy fulfilled. She stepped forward, brushed his lips with hers, furtively, always shy at first. Smiling, she caressed his cheek, rubbed away the wrinkles under his eye with her thumb. She took him by the waist, molded herself against him, eyes closed, nestled her chin in his neck, breathing, inhaling his smell, which made her heady, almost physically drunk. She led him to the living room, where she offered him the green satin sofa, facing the orange satin sofa and the white satin curtains. Lit from below, the green plants were shadowed on the ceiling, a Hollywood jungle. And the portrait of Christopher Isherwood stared at him, his blue eyes bleeding with the pain of all those years of living and knowing things that he still could not share. Under the portrait, the purple armchair offered the streamline curve of its bamboo trimming, while close to her lover, close to the sofa where he sat comfortably, attentive to her mood, her look of today, the two mushroom stools were available to the impatient talker. But she chose to kneel at his feet, her arms in turn folded on his knees, curved around his waist, or one arm extended on his wrist, on his shoulder, fingers inside his shirt collar, caressing negligently the neck she loved.

She desired him and he knew it, but she wanted to postpone for as long as she could the moment when she would tip over into this second state when mad euphoria would waltz her away, overtake her will, tumble her into a somersault where no nets were stretched to the rescue, to leave her in peace of mind and limb, contented like a well-fed dog sleeping in the sun.

She spoke with animation, sure of his loving attention, of his indulgence to her babbling.

"I came home late—eight-thirty—today is Friday," she specified, "you know what my neighborhood is like on weekends—everyone's gone. Even my concierge 'veekens.' Even our alley cats are driven off in wicker baskets to better weeds, freer trees. You can't get a haircut on a Saturday, let alone buy bread; you could die of starvation. The place is clean-swept—deserted. Humans and animals have transported their lives elsewhere." She stopped for inspiration. "It has been raining, do you know? For hours," she added, "pouring at first, now just a lazy weekend drizzle." She jumped up and went to look out of the window, parting the curtains. "I must tell you something funny that happened earlier. I went to buy your birthday present." She smiled at him to see the effect of this news. Yes, he was pleased, touched even. She came back close to him. "I was late from the doctor's, so my friend (you have to have a friend at Cartier's, or else) had gone home already. What to do in the six o'clock deluge, rue de Rivoli? A car stopped. The window unwound. . . . Shall I continue or am I just blowing hot air?" She waited for the answer, which didn't come. Her voice dwindled away. "Never mind, I got your present." She walked up and down nervously, unable to continue this absurd pretense anymore. She turned off all the lights. It was easier in the dark.

"As I told you earlier, I came home late. Eight-thirty, and my rich neighborhood is weekending. Even our alley cats are weekending; only the florist downstairs was still open, hoping for the last forty francs of the day (no, make it twenty-five in this foul weather), and the café across the street. One customer only. A bearded chap, trying to be jolly all by himself in the empty café, at eight-thirty on a rainy Friday night. I tried to imagine you sitting next to me, how we would watch the waiters going through the locking-up routine, what we would say, how we would nudge each other and speak from the corners of our mouths. "The *patron* himself is emptying the sugar bowl. Do you think he counts the sugar lumps? The zinc was being polished—by the way, it is made of brass, not zinc—and shining like gold under the dirty napkin. A customer came in for a *ballon de rouge*. He wasn't encouraged to stay, that was obvious. Someone who gets the place to himself can become trouble. Meanwhile, the neon-lit menu, two foot by one foot and a half, was brought in, the outside chairs piled up, the tables Siamese-twinned one on top of the other, not brought in yet out of respect for us, their two customers. Over there, at the far corner, a waiter leaned the tables against the banquette, crudely upturned the chairs, revealing their underbellies, getting ready to sweep the sawdust and cigarette butts. Two flat-footed Algerians came in for coffee, but who cares about them? Not the waiter. I ate my dinner, watching.

"Finally the bearded customer crawled away, escaping

from the oppressive loneliness of this place, while assuring the *patron* that he had really enjoyed his *brandade de morue*–'long time since I ate one–so good–really–and thanks.' See him backing away with each word, for fear the *patron* might offer *un petit cognac*. But all was well. Time was tic-tocking on the wall clock, it was obvious no other customer would venture in. It was time for the kitchen staff to leave, one by one, like the musicians in that symphony (who by? I forget).

"First the Spanish lady who prepares *oeuf mayonnaise, salades, et sandwiches*. During the day she presents a girlish sight, covered as she is in Swissly demure flowers, but now, decorous as a Catholic duenna going to confession, except for the missing mantilla, she is molded in black veils, polyester, though, not silk.

"The assistant cook leaves next, pale and wan, a student burdened by the weight of metaphysical problems. One looks for books under his arm, there aren't any, the disguise is not complete.

"And finally the chef himself, always an Algerian in these neighborhood cafés. A sorrowful face, lined with crevasses deep enough to figure on the map of the Atlas range, he comes out of the kitchen dressed in the best of English casuals, red silk handkerchief tucked in the Harris tweed breast pocket. A banker after his ticker-tape machine has stopped would wear nothing else. Because he is *le chef*, he shakes hands only with *le patron*, dismissing the waiters with a wave. '*Noblesse oblige*.'

"I've often wondered: Is the work done for our benefit by those in uniform so painful and demeaning that off working hours they have to assume another identity, just as artificial but played in earnest this time? And is this identity imagined just for the moment when they walk across the emptying café to shake hands with the *patron*, recognizable only by the exhaustion worn on their faces? Or does this disguise last all night and Sundays too? Does the chef sleep in silk pajamas, his initials embroidered over his heart? Or does he go home to feed his rabbits in faded jeans?

"Finally the waiter in my empty section gestures with a thumb toward the door; the *patron* nods yes, and oh, precious French economy, the last remaining *baguettes* are cut in two and fitted in the ice-cream freezer that is wheeled in.

"Although I was only finishing my brie and would have liked a cup of coffee, I understood the signals and tactfully asked for the check. I was sent into the wet night with heartless indifference.

" '*Bonne soirée, madame!*'

"I cared because I knew that now I would never hear the last orders mumbled by the *patron* to the waiter, or the sharp locking of the doors, or alas, see what disguise the *patron* himself assumes when he leaves his job."

She stopped talking, depressed. There was no more to tell. She looked for a long time toward the empty couch. The game didn't work anymore. She decided that she had better get to work. What was the alternative? She went to her writing table, switched on the reading lamp, and sat down. She started to read her last unfinished story. At first there was such a vacuum inside her, even alone she was ashamed of her ineptitude. In front of those terrible pages, she had to admit that she hardly existed. A breath, a speck of dust, nothing consistent.

But little by little she followed the sense of the words, which formed a story, where people had names, moved, and she would make them move further if she wanted to. Suddenly, like the diver poised on the board, who has already in his mind run through the whole muscular exploit to its conclusion before trusting himself in the air, she saw with certitude the new sentence form itself, full, specific, infinitely denser. She wrote:

"When she came home around one-thirty from a thrilling evening, Meg thought to herself, I must buy some new underwear, I think something is about to happen; yes, at last Meg had met someone really interesting. . . ."

Not much, but a start all the same. Hunched over the page, one shoulder higher than the other, her loneliness now broken in, invaded by welcomed apparitions, presences, she went on writing in the spot of light. It was going to be a productive night after all.

Claudine Goes Home

This time it was because Greg forgot to bring home her particular brand of cigarettes. But as usual, that small detail was only the starting block for everything else. Meg, especially when she had a glass of whiskey in her hand, was incapable of having a fight in the singular. All the old beefs were thrown in and she was practicing real good on the new ones. She was specially revved up about New York, her voracious yearning for the theater, the smart restaurants, and, of course, shopping. Only in New York could a woman be smartly dressed, New York where her childhood friends lived, her mother too, and all of what made life bearable.

Claudine took the portable TV to the kitchen. She, too, was watching a good belting out, but "I Love Lucy" had more laughs. Only problem was, Greg felt obliged to carry the heavy box for his little girl, so Meg followed into the kitchen, intensifying the yelling.

Claudine discovered long ago that the only way to have some quiet when things started up was to go to the upstairs bathroom and turn all the taps on. The cascade of water made her dream of beaches, where her daddy had taught her to plunge fearlessly into the breaking waves. And another magic trick: Dracula teeth hooked in a mouth distorted by a snarl, eyes half closed, her hands clawing at an imaginary victim, Claudine dreamed of bloody revenge.

Meg has seen to it that Claudine has every possible goody that Saks, Magnin's, and Bullock's can offer a little girl of eight. She wakes up to her clock radio, possesses the usual transistor, record player, and tape recorder, has piles of T-shirts to choose from and the company of an eight-foot giraffe casting a fixed glass eye at the artificial flowers climbing up the wallpaper. But motherly love extends no further: Claudine has to fix her own breakfast. In no way will Meg get up at that ungodly hour of seven and prepare those dumb cereals, the glass of milk, or whatever else the little darling has decided to eat. Claudine prides herself on being imaginative: a cold taco and Meg's leftover whiskey from last night will do just fine this morning. Nothing smarter than to announce to the class that you've had your ration for the day. On her way out from the kitchen she sometimes bumps into Daddy, who gives her a dollar, out of guilt, she figures, and then off she goes to school on a choice of locomotion: depending on what time it is, her mood, and the weather, it is either roller skates, skateboard, or bicycle with flying pennant.

That Monday, when she came home at four, Meg gave her the news, full blast right in the smacker: "Honey, I'm getting rid of your dad, I can't stand him anymore. No consideration is all I get. I'm a very attractive woman, you can see that plainly even at your age, and all my friends agree that I have a swell figure. He must be running around . . . the only way to explain it. Yeah, they all have a secretary tucked away somewhere; that's classic, my friends warned me." After a few moments while she mulled over her bitterness in silence, she offered this eloquent conclusion: "Only sweet word he's said to me since Christmas is that I have pretty feet. Big deal!"

Although she didn't bother to understand the details of her mother's argument, Claudine caught the main idea. Her father's suitcases piled up in the hall, with his tennis rackets and golf clubs leaning against them, were clear enough.

"You're divorcing Daddy?" "You bet I am" was the direct reply. Claudine took in the glass of whiskey, the rage manifest in every part of her mother's comportment. She had noticed long ago that Meg always wore floating clothes when she was angry. No belt or zipper could resist her. Also at those moments she would kick off her shoes wherever she was, as if her anger needed complete freedom to express itself.

Meg thought: Well, now I told her, and she's taken it very well. You never know what to expect from children. It is true that Claudine was unusually quiet for three days, but on the fourth day, right in the middle of recess, she started belting poor Julie Nichols, who had done nothing at all except bump into her. She hit her ferociously, with all the strength of her little fists, kicking her too, and using every four-letter word in the book. "The foulest language the school has ever heard," or so Mrs. Puttman, the principal, proclaimed indignantly to Claudine's mother. "I can't imagine where she learned those words," she added, pinched-lipped. The scandal cooled down only because Claudine was such a bright student and Mrs. Puttman suggested earnestly that Claudine be given tranquilizers under the supervision of Dr. Moore. She said fits of hostility happened to children who were growing too fast or not fast enough, she couldn't remember which, called it a chemical imbalance. Little John Fowler was given those pills and was generally calm unless his mother forgot to give them to him in the morning. Meg promised to take Claudine to Dr. Moore.

Now that Daddy was gone, they were often alone at dinner and Meg would try to talk to Claudine. In bursts of reproaches and complaints she would try to justify to herself, to Claudine, and for the general rectification of Right the urgent necessity to eliminate her husband from their lives. By inference, she hoped Claudine would not be upset by the sudden disappearance of her daddy. But of course she achieved the opposite. Claudine buried her affection for her father in the armor-plated vault of her heart, where her mother's words could not reach it.

"Your father could have had a great career," Meg would start, "and look what he's become: the owner of a Laundromat chain. I ask you, is that a career for a Harvard man?" Faced with her daughter's skeptical little face, she would think: That child doesn't care, that's all; and she'd explain all the more why she had to take the final step. "At first he was fun, he was interested in things, wanted to see all the shows on Broadway. You see, we received the New York *Times* then, but after he bought out the chain in the valley, he canceled the paper, said he didn't have time to read it and that it just gave me all sorts of ideas. That was a real blow, I don't mind telling you." An answer from her daughter wasn't really necessary, so she went on: "Of course, I still kept up the subscription, but now I have to pay for it out of my own pocket. When I married your father, before I said yes, I made him swear he'd take me to New York every year. Hell, look how he's kept his promise, I haven't gone for three years!"

Meg was so engrossed in her train of thought that she didn't notice, after Claudine had escaped to watch TV in the den, that her paper napkin was torn to shreds and rolled in a little ball, tighter than a bullet.

She didn't notice either that the enamel coffee spoons had disappeared, and the escargot set and those silver-plated salt shakers she used only for grand sit-down dinners, which she had given so rarely lately, because Greg always complained of being tired at night and said that those formal dinners bored the bejesus out of him.

Effie was the one to notice. She came three times a week in her '73 fuchsia Cadillac and was very touchy about things like that. She would raid the icebox; there never were any cookies left in the jar, and the whiskey was definitely down one notch after she was gone, but she didn't want anyone to suspect her of stealing. She reported the strange missings to Meg "because I don't want no one to think that I taken them." But Meg didn't pay attention, she didn't care now, she had bigger things on her mind. Jack Wishpart, her lawyer, was negotiating for the alimony, and can you believe it, Greg was talking about selling the house. "No way!" was her answer to that. Let him sell a few Laundromats if he needed money to pay the mortgage and the alimony and child support, or buy a few more, for all she cared. But she was not going to let him sell her beautiful Beverly Hills home. What next? Did he want her to be locked up in an apartment with that live wire of a child? She was irate at the thought and would have liked to tell someone, Claudine for instance. But Claudine was nowhere to be seen these days. "Where is that child anyway? Always racing around on her bicycle."

One of her friends said that she spotted her on the beach. You only saw her at mealtimes and then she didn't talk, didn't even listen, just had that absent look on her freckled face.

At school Claudine had been despondent at first and ashamed to admit that her mom was divorcing Daddy. But the kids explained a thing or two that gave it a whole different slant. First of all, they made it plain that divorced parents were a real good deal.

"You get everything twice, two birthdays, two Christmases, and so on, and then if you're clever you bid one against the other, get it? You tell your dad that your mom is going to give you a Seiko; always start with your dad, though, and he'll feel he has to give you a pony or something bigger than your mom. Your dad's your best giver, because he's not at home and he worries. You can always make him cough up five dollars or so by telling him that your mom forgot to give you pocket money."

That was one thing, and Claudine had to agree that it worked out that way, especially when Dad, on his days out with Claudine, brought along that big klutz, this Susan with the big boom-booms. She was always talking about herself, the dummy, and sometimes in the third person like a baby, which embarrassed Daddy no end.

But Claudine had something else going. She had started her own business and it was thriving, thanks to an active trade going on at school. Georgie Snarler had this big brother who bought anything you had to sell, hence the coffee spoons, escargot set, etc. He had a car and a garage, so it was a cinch to sell him anything, bicycles even, and on weekends Beverly Hills was full of bicycles. Of course it was smarter to go to another neighborhood if you worked the alleys. Early in the morning or at night were your best times. Claudine had never been caught yet, although once she came pretty near. She had to pretend she thought it was her own, and thank Buster Keaton she never lost her nerve.

When her pockets were full, she would go to her toy closet, and inside her dollhouse was her secret cashbox. Claudine would recite her special incantation before opening it:

> "Abraham, Washington, and Jackson too,
> You got to grow and milliontiply,
> Or else I'll put the curse on you,
> And pierce your eyes so you will die!"

She'd do a few gestures, something like those she saw the Pope do on TV when all the crowd in that foreign country would go down on their knees and look like they'd just seen a flying saucer. No need to go on about it. Claudine was doing real well.

Although making money was fun, life was just not the same at home. She couldn't get used to Daddy's having to make an appointment on the phone in order to see her. Once he had tried to barge in to talk Mom out of going in front of the judge. He'd rung the bell for a while, 'cause naturally Mom had changed all the locks, and when he saw that Meg was walled in her fortress like the English at Orleans (lessons have a way of sticking like transfers on real-life events), Dad got the ladder from the garage and leaned it against the house to climb in through the bathroom window. He got in all right, but Mom got in the bathroom too and tried to push him back out and Dad slapped her so hard that she backed away into her collection of perfume bottles and that started a real humdinger of a fight. They were knocking each other all over the place, bouncing off the walls so hard that the towel racks were pulled off and the place reeked of mixed perfume and they were crunching bath salts and glass and Mom was yelling, panting, and screaming until they both saw Claudine, white as a sheet, watching silently, and only then did they give up. No one could have stopped Claudine from racing to the beach on her bike and weeping bitterly, weeping for Daddy who didn't know the right way to put some sense into Mom, weeping for the end of good times, and later weeping and hiccuping because she was very hungry, so that she had searched for something to eat, which she hadn't found, and had eventually settled on smoking cigarette butts she picked up in the sand.

The other time when things got really hairy was when she had come home early because the heating had broken down all over school and it got so cold, yeah, well, California cold, that everybody had been sent home after lunch, not that anyone minded, the general feeling being that it was a lucky break. So Claudine had decided that this was just the right time to go on a "grabble and scramble" binge with Judy Webster, her best friend. They had come out of Woolworth's the victorious possessors of the most elephantine pair of pink cotton panties, so large that they could each slip through one leg and skate home like Siamese twins, laughing enough to bust your guts. But when she got home with her pink trophy, drunk with pride like a soldier after looting, she stopped short in her tracks. What were those strange animal moans coming from upstairs? At first she thought that there was a murder going on on her mother's TV, but when she stood at the door, just ajar, of her mother's bedroom, what she saw made her head spin and beaded her forehead with cold sweat. She felt so suddenly sick that she had to rush to her bathroom and vomit. She knew that the groaning woman lying naked on her back with her knees bent like a beetle pinned on a board was her mother. No, not possible, not her mother—yes, her very own mother; but that fleshy man who seemed to hit her viciously with his contracted pelvis, holding her mother's wrists in a vise so tight that that woman, her mother, seemed to be clawing at his hands, she didn't know him, couldn't tell who, didn't have time to recognize. She only knew with certainty that it was not her father. She sped on her bicycle to Judy Webster's home, where she was sick several more times in the secrecy of Judy's bathroom. Later Mrs. Webster called Meg to say that the little girls were playing sweetly upstairs with Judy's new Barbie doll, and couldn't Claudine stay the night? Claudine never explained to her friend why she cried during the night, right after waking up from a nightmare, but friends don't need to be told and Judy was a good friend. She took Claudine into her own bed, enfolding her in her arms, and waited for her breathing to get slow and even before she finally let herself drift into sleep.

Claudine never forgot witnessing the unmentionable scene. She always kept the image in front of her eyes when talking to her mother and inwardly questioned every man she came close to, comparing his form to that one engraved in her memory, her curiosity scanning slyly from the back to the front bulge of their trousers. Once she followed a man who had gone to hide behind some trees in the Beverly Hills park, hoping she would see or understand the awesome mystery. The man tried to lose her and finally left the park without doing whatever he was looking to do. Claudine was ashamed of her voyeurism, she felt guilty and knew that the man understood what she was after. She knew she was trespassing over adult knowledge, and yet never could stop wondering. Claudine had lost her innocence.

Suddenly things went very fast. One morning Meg got up at the same time as Claudine, poured herself a whiskey right after coffee, and when Claudine came home that afternoon Mom announced that that was it, she was free at last: "A good thing done and good riddance!"

Claudine wasn't too sure what her mother had meant. She didn't dare ask because she didn't want to hear what she feared most, so she went and talked about it to Judy Webster, who said that to divorce you had to go to court every day for at least a week, witness the case of Rosy Harris's parents; that in any case, nothing was lost because your average husband and wife get married again, even after a real complete divorce. Claudine thought to herself: You never know with Mom, better get things settled and fixed up now, before it's too late. That evening she went up to her cashbox and after going through her usual hocus-pocus counted her stack of bank notes.

She came downstairs slowly, full of resentment at adult foolishness, and deposited her offering for the good of matrimonial reconciliation.

"Here you are, Mom, here's $927.25. Now you don't need to divorce Daddy, you can go to New York, and don't worry, I can make this much bread every year, easy. If you want my opinion, Dad's not crazy about that divorce idea anyway, so now he can come home, okay?"

Of course, Claudine had not foreseen the strict logical consequences of her act. Her mother's reaction was sharp and to the point: "(A) I'm divorced, as of today; (b) I have no intention of getting back with Daddy-o; and (c) where the hell did you get all that money?"

Claudine was profoundly humiliated. Her infallible plan hadn't worked. Not only had her generosity been cruelly overlooked, but she was being punished for it, insomuch as Mom had grabbed the loot but not invited Daddy back. The pain remained. In fact the longing for her father became more poignant now that she knew for certain that her mom wouldn't change her mind. She tried to get help from Judy Webster, who had no wise solution to offer, and in the solitude of her nights Claudine told her giraffe, who listened with the same indifferent astonishment. Its cuddly fur warmed by the proximity of the radiator was Claudine's only solace.

Now that the divorce was over, Meg needed a change of pace. She looked around for a new orientation. She had fulfilled her wish, her wrathful revenge was now executed. She was even surprised at how easy it had been to get this man down on his knees. When she recapitulated all the rounds she had lost in her years of marriage, gone down crying before the second bell, she was surprised at her newly discovered power. So that was it, all you had to do was call the referee, a lawyer, and the enemy was dragged out, vilified, punished, made to pay for every male prerogative he had ever enjoyed over her, for having had a good time at the office, for having forced her to listen to and admire his endlessly boring business maneuvers, for having been too tired when she felt like it, and mostly for having lost the eager courtesy of their courtship days. In short, for being the husband when she was only the wife. But now, what next? What was she, Meg, going to do with the forty or so victorious years left to her life?

First, thought Meg, I must be constructive, rebuild my life on a more gracious pattern, favorable to inner development: I must breathe, enjoy, expand. New York, New

York, is the answer! She had visions of parties at the exhibitions of young painters, drinks with the famous after an opening night. I can still get into my size 12 dresses, she thought. Sunday afternoons at the Metropolitan Museum with a young poet would be delightful: I'll offer dinner afterward, the Ginger Man is not too expensive. She saw in front of her the mirage of a new life shimmering, glittering, wrapped in the vaporous pink gauze of illusion.

Of her daughter's future she thought little. Claudine would follow and that was that. There were plenty of good schools in New York, in fact the child, too, would flourish at the contact of sophistication.

The house was up for sale after all. Once it was sold, they'd be in clover, but for the time being it would be fun to slum it a little, like two young girls landing in New York for the first time.

New York it was. Claudine, under some kind of cultural shock, tried bravely, but nothing of hers fitted in this new town. Her clothes were much too thin; her accent, which the kids at the new school made fun of, excluded her from the smart set. She didn't get the lingo. Anyway, her identity, molded in the rays of the California sun, was too candid for this urban guerrilla school ground. Of all her treasures she had rescued only her cashbox, empty and desecrated now without its mystic chapel: her dollhouse. She had also lost her engines of power: her roller skates, skateboard, and bicycle. And where was the tight curve around the camellia bush that she used to hug with Olympic grace, right knee almost touching the ground? And the sidewalks that she commanded her steed to jump, wheels one foot off the cement? She missed her father, her school friends, her giraffe even, and yes, Effie and her '73 fuchsia

Cadillac, even though there never was any chocolate cake left after she was gone. Claudine wanted to go back home.

She took the subway as far as the line would take her and then got out. She was in the suburbs somewhere. She started walking until she saw a Greyhound station. That seemed a good idea. She opened the glass door.

The first employee she talked to seemed interested. He watched Claudine with keen blue eyes while he questioned her.

"What gave you the fine idea to ask me?"

Then he added thoughtfully, "What about your mother? Haven't you got a mother?"

"Sort of, yeah. But my dad's waiting for me in L.A."

"Waiting for you? He knows you're coming?"

"Sure he knows."

"How come he didn't send you the money if he's waiting for you?" he said, looking down at her feet to see if she had any luggage. She was caught lying.

"Well, okay. It's a surprise. I want to surprise him."

"But your mother? What about your mother?" he repeated.

"She doesn't care. Won't bother her if I'm gone. She's too busy running around and stuff."

He looked at Claudine with some sort of wild kick dancing in his eyes.

"Yeah, mothers. Don't tell me," he said enigmatically, and then, his thin lips keeping tight control over his teeth, he made a sudden decision.

"Well, I'll take care of you. You just sit pretty and wait for me."

She sat in a tired armchair that had once expressed the

same streamlined energy that the Greyhound bus still liked to portray. She looked around her with curiosity. Sitting in the next armchair was an anemic-looking young mother, the kind who gets caught every time with a slobbering brat, wrestles with him all day until he falls into a deadweight sleep. A black man was sleeping on a couch, badly shod, emaciated and breathing out cheap alcoholic fumes, his dog-eared fake-leather suitcase used as a pillow. A couple of Mexicans were waiting too, staring straight ahead. Claudine had seen that same look of respectful patience in the gardener's eyes. The woman was overweight, congested in neon-colored garments. It was depressing all right. Claudine waited for about an hour. Nobody seemed to pay much attention to her except for him, the guy in the gray uniform.

Every time she looked in the direction of the ticket counter, she met those limpid blue eyes. He was always busy, seemed to be fussing with papers, though he wasn't selling tickets; he had something else to do, she didn't know what. He looked at his watch often and had a nervous way of checking that his hair was razor-sharp neatly in place.

Just as Claudine was looking down on the old linoleum floor, thinking, "Jesus, I could do with a Coke," she noticed a pair of men's feet that were unusually small. She looked up: the man with the blue eyes was standing right there in front of her.

"Do you want to go to the ladies' room before we go? There is a john on the bus, but I always think it's more comfortable here. Down the hall on the left," he said as she got up. "We're leaving soon."

That's right, she thought, the bus must be leaving soon. She had noticed that the place was getting crowded and luggage had been piling up in the corner.

She did as he suggested, went to the toilet. He was waiting close to the door when she came out. She had a funny feeling that he had been watching her in there; just the look he gave her. He was holding a Coke in one hand and something else in the other, she couldn't tell what.

"Come with me," he said sharply.

They weaved through the suitcase-encumbered crowd and came out the back way. There were several buses, dirty and seemingly abandoned, parked in front of the gas pumps. It was starting to get dark now; there was no one around, but Claudine didn't pay attention. The man led her silently. He opened the door of the bus with a key hanging in a bunch at the end of a strong metallic chain. When he helped her get up the tall steps his hands were nervous and thin, gripping her arm in a way that hurt.

"I'm letting you in first," he said; "I've reserved the whole back row for you. Isn't that nice of me? We can't put the lights on, it would use up the batteries. You'd better lie down and sleep, so no one will see you. Here," he said, squeezing the Coke and what she now recognized as a chocolate bar into her hand, "No one can say Mike's not a nice guy. Right, kid? You just lie down now." And he added, backing away as if he knew what she was thinking, "No one will find you before we leave, don't worry."

She felt very uncomfortable alone in the dark bus with him. Secretly she wished she could go home now. She turned to ask him how long was the drive to L.A., but it was too late; he was already locking the door.

When she came back home from a thrilling evening, around one-thirty in the morning, Meg thought to herself: I must buy some new underwear, I think something's about to happen. Yes, at last she had met someone really interesting.

Meg noticed that the bathroom was unusually neat, just as she had left it, in fact. No dirty socks, panties, or sneakers lying about. As soon as she entered the kitchen to get ice water for her sleeping pill, she smelled the burned TV dinner she had left in the oven for Claudine. Her note was still on the Formica table and there were no dirty dishes or glasses lying around. She rushed to Claudine's room and found the bed untouched. For a fleeting moment she was annoyed that something should go wrong on this auspicious night. "Just like her to give me headaches when things are going nicely." She tried to imagine "where that funny kid had gone." A late-night movie? No, there was TV for that. To sleep over with a school friend? A boy maybe? No, not that yet. Claudine was still at the age when you thought boys were pimply and smelly. She searched around for a clue and found nothing. It was so late, she felt she couldn't call Claudine's friends; anyway she realized she didn't know if Claudine had made any. "That kid is so sneaky, you never know what she's up to." Still, Meg felt the need to call someone. But who? Claudine's father? The police? Hospitals? Her own mother? But that relationship was somewhat strained, now that she lived in New York permanently. She decided to call Greg. He would take charge. He should, in fact.

As the phone kept ringing its frail jingle across all that expanse of fertile land and arid desert, Meg was painfully reminded that Claudine was her only link with tender feelings and intimacy. She had no one else really. An inner voice kept nagging her to the rhythm of the ringing. Suddenly she remembered the time. "Oh sure, it's ten-thirty in Los Angeles, Greg is eating out."

So she called the police. A female operator with a nasal Brooklyn accent took down Claudine's description with routine indifference. When Meg remarked on this, the woman answered, bored, "Listen, lady, we get about two hundred calls every night. Phone us back if she turns up; some of those kids do when they want a square meal." She didn't sound hopeful.

When the phone rang next to her ear, Meg was lying on the bed fully dressed. She was jarred back from troubled slumber, so it took her a while to understand the man.

His voice was hysterical to the point of singing; harsh and loud with anger and then, after a while, intimate, almost cooing with tenderness.

"Oh yes, I understood just how she felt. You see, my mother left me just a while ago." He added, syncopating the syllables, as if stabbing them, "How-could-you-do-that-to-her-you-bitch?" Suddenly he hung up.

They found the body three days later, hidden in the brambles behind the Greyhound garage. Naked, her body revealed the athletic form of the determined child she had been, with just a hint of shape to come around the hips. They arrested a young man with porcelain-blue eyes, Mike Mazersky, who had just started working for Greyhound. Now that his mother was dead he lived alone in the unkempt tenement flat. His clothes were strewn around the apartment carelessly, but they found the pile of Claudine's clothes in the only closet, next to his mother's, neatly washed and ironed, not hanging on hangers but folded, as if ready to be packed in a suitcase for a trip. Several awkward poems scribbled in a childish handwriting were inserted between the folds of cloth, tender warnings against the harsh weather, syrupy rhymes, reminders of his obsessional love. A faint stale odor of mold lingered on the shelves.

The neighbors explained that his mother had died about three years ago and that Mike had been very much on his own ever since.

The Dullard

While she was carefully running the razor over her leg, removing the shaving cream in strips, which oddly enough reminded her of dear Daddy sitting on his lawn mower of a Saturday, green stretches behind him combed in pleasing rectilinear strips, she kept alert to the sounds in the main room. Was Cy doing his work all right? You never knew with that man. This morning she had asked him to sew a missing button on her white shirt, washed in the machine last night, and iron it, too, so that she could wear it to work. Most mornings he would have done it readily enough; this morning, inexplicably, he had rebelled just like a mule that suddenly refuses to step over a small stick or walk in the shadow of a dark tree. Yes, she thought, Cy had an affinity with mules. At times he was reasonable enough, but occasionally he was obstinately opposed to her requests. It depended on his store of affability, or his degree of understanding of what life was all about. For a man with such regular habits he could be very unexpected at times.

All she had asked this morning, apart from getting her shirt ready, was that he should add up the expenditures of the month and balance their checkbooks. After all, this was the end of the month, what could be more sensible? She had not liked his answer: "Maybe, if I have the time."

Every morning Cy and Millie got up at five-thirty so that Cy could do the household chores before going to the office and Millie would go through her detailed toilet; this was the way it was understood between them. Millie was one of those women who needed long hours every morning to reconstruct the world into something seemly and neat, clear of any mysteries that might baffle her understanding, so that the day would not bring back or carry forward the lingering desolation of her nights (yes, most mornings she woke up with a throat full of tears, ready to weep in grieving for she knew not what, or whom, tears that had accumulated during the night for the moment when she might question herself, if she only would admit her sorrow). Every morning, then, she gave birth to a world that any Republican, such as her father, could explain in simple parlance, his world, with just a dash of liberalism thrown in to bring it up to date. And liberal she certainly was; did she not work for a black boss?

While Cy sewed and ironed and got little Jeannie out of bed and ready for her school bus, he switched on the news and Millie heard in the bathroom what she already knew, namely, that this morning the world was again on the verge of disaster, due for imminent collapse because people and the government, too, were irresponsible and irrational; this country was threatened every morning by acts of single or mass terrorism, even though the taxes were high enough to pay a decent police system to keep all those insubordinate people, minority groups, and sex offenders in check, but no, owing to a weakness inherent in this permissive society, they were incapable of handling it. Millie stopped her razor in midair.

"What fools they all are to get into such a fix!" she thought and, smiling, resumed shaving every unseemly hair so that her limbs would remain perfectly glabrous throughout the day. Later she calmly drew above her eyes two thick assertive curves where nature had only sketched timid eyebrows, puffed out her blond hair, which grew so limp, especially in this tropical climate, but first she fed her pallid skin with creams and moisturizers and foundation, as she read the stars did when filming, and rouge and blue where it was called for; now the pleasing painting was fixed with powder, and lastly, slowly and patiently, every one of her lashes was waxed, lovingly coated, so that each strand stood up rigid and thick as if made out of nylon and the effect every time she blinked slowly was as if she were rolling down the blinds.

She didn't quite know why she did this every morning; it wasn't because she loved herself and took pleasure in embellishing something already quite beautiful—she didn't even think that the finished result was an improvement—it was more out of a sense of duty, a respect for tradition handed down to girls through their mothers' fashion magazines, as if now that arms and legs and breasts could be exposed no female face should ever be seen naked, for it might reveal something not quite decent, something shocking like the bewilderment that overtook her very soul at the end of the day after coming home from the office, some witchcraft taking hold with the advancing shadows, when only a whiskey could dull this inexplicable anxiety about nothing she cared to define. But in the mornings when the mask was applied, smooth and glossy, her appearance re-created, she felt safe again. Now she could correct what was wrong with the world, starting with Cy and little Jeannie, because everything was in focus, framed by her coated lashes; she knew the right answers, took the right decisions.

She came out of the bathroom serene, neat, and embalmed, seated herself at the breakfast table with a righteous slide of her hips, waiting for Cy to serve her. She always watched Jeannie's manners severely; unable to differentiate between breaches of etiquette and criminal transgression, her scale of punishment was accordingly irrational. The child had long ago learned to make up her own rules. Millie turned her tolerant gaze on Cy and asked him if he had fulfilled the duties she had assigned to him. He looked at her quizzically and answered, "No, I haven't," and that was all.

Understanding and patient as she might be, she had to admit that her husband was sometimes quite peculiar for a man who could only be described as inept. Normally he was sedate to the point of eccentricity. For years now he had carried out his marital duties punctually on Saturday nights, whether the two of them went out or stayed home, after a dinner at the restaurant, a dance at the disco, or after the cinema no matter what they had seen, a love story, a murder mystery, or a comedy, or even after two hours of tedium in front of the TV if there was nothing else going on that Saturday night; even if he had the flu he would perform conscientiously the routine function. Millie developed a dull anger against this ritual, regular as the cuckoo in a Swiss clock. She would go through her evening toilet as any decent respectable woman should, but on most Saturday nights she defeated her own sexual frustrations, snapping at him, making contemptuous cracks at what she called his "hygienic exercise." Cy would resign himself and calmly drop off to sleep. Some Saturdays Millie would drink several more whiskeys than usual, so as to pass out and avoid the dreariness of pay day.

On weeknights when her whiskey level was just high enough to relieve her of her inhibitions, she would lie awake in bed and allow her imagination to wander toward the same disturbing longings: her eyes closed, she loved to fancy that she shared her bed with an unknown man, someone she had never met, had not seen the face or the body of, but could only guess at in the semi-obscurity, whose musky perfume and dense muscular flesh suggested rough passion. A slow exploration of her body with hands at once callous and yet sensitive would first arouse her senses; and when, enfevered by this sweet rhythmical stroking, her whole impatient body had reached such painful delirium, a pitch of such frenzy, that she would moan and cry out in her phantasm, she would plead for him to grab her fleshy buttocks and enter his hot dagger into her, forcefully, so that she would gasp with surprise and fear. Cy never woke up during the acting out of her fantasies, even when she relieved herself of the plethoric tension knotting her belly.

A heavy mammal beached on her bed; her panting would decrease little by little to fall into rhythm with the quiet breathing of her husband, before she would drop off to sleep.

She would have denied it if anyone had reminded her of their courtship days when, seized by uncontrollable desire, Cy and Millie would make love in his run-down Volkswagen, or on a hot day under a tree in a public park, or again early one evening on a secluded beach, it mattered little where or what the danger was in those days—she would have denied it because she had wiped such intemperate incidents from her memory, since the time when they had opened their first bank account, bought the new car now that he held a job and the baby was on its way, which was why, with the consent and encouragement of dear Daddy, she had decided to marry Cy.

She often thought that she would not have done so had she known then what he would turn out to be; Cy had not kept his side of the bargain. When they had settled down to marry he had agreed that they must now observe a certain decorum, had even commended her for her refinement, her genteel breeding. He used to say to friends in front of her, with a touch of teasing mingled with pride, "There's no beating my girl for minding her P's and Q's."

But little by little the gentle irony of his quips had acquired an edge, he had become frankly hostile and lately indifferent and vague. For years now he had tried to avoid the daily responsibilities and it was left to her to remind him:

"This is Saturday, dear, remember to have the car washed"—"We're Thursday, dear, remember? The laundry is ready at the cleaners"—and every thirty-first of March, "April Fool's Day tomorrow, dear, and who's the fool? The one who forgets to fill in his income tax return." It was endless.

But she would forgive his slackness in assuming the necessary details of life—after all, men are forgetful—if only he didn't embarrass her constantly. He would forget every time, and this enraged her, to light her cigarette; she was forever waiting with an unlit cigarette between her fingers, and when they were out in the car he would sooner slam the door in her face than open it for her. And he would always get into a huddle with uninteresting people at parties, the kind that will never go places because they are quite content as they are. In a corner, together with what she called his football team, Cy would tell tall fishing stories, guffaw at his own punch lines, drink too much, and altogether act as if he had nothing better to do in life than have fun. Personally, she thought that this display of childish horseplay was vulgar. If she took the trouble to introduce him to an eminent faculty friend of her daddy's, Cy would emit his usual evasive grunts, nod from time to time with a pained quizzical expression, and eventually shuffle off without having said a word. Oh, he was maddening! And it didn't help their social status that his hair should be so short. How can you expect to be promoted when you run an electric razor all over your head every fortnight? She thought he looked like a convict, especially as his skin was scabrous as orange peel, the texture left over from his juvenile acne.

She would say to Johnny May, the maid, who came twice a week to do the heavy work, "He's not a bad man really, just doesn't impress anyone. Johnny May, I married a dullard." And she would sigh, "Oh dear, you would never believe it, last night I came into the kitchen while he was preparing dinner, you know I can't cook that Caribbean stuff, so I leave it to him, can you picture this: he had the radio on and he was dancing Reggae while chopping up the onions, now, where would he have learned that silly dance?"

Johnny May, revealing her golden tooth in a sweet smile, would say: "Mr. Cy, he know a lot of things."

Outside, the tropical storm swelled up, the wind blew capriciously on the long palm leaves, flexing them into curves gracious as Balinese dancers' hands, willing the trunks of younger trees to bend until they lamented with pain, raveling the long loose creepers into new loops, and when the pall of humid vapors had reached saturation, as if called to silence by the baton of an invisible conductor, the random concert of bullfrogs, crickets, birds, and that insect the cicada, who exists, as so many people do, only to produce a noise totally out of proportion to its size and function, all suspended sound and stood expectant, listening for the first drop of rain; it falls the size of a bird's egg, slackly, on a large leaf; the next one follows and the next one and soon the heavy drops fall so densely that the forest vibrates with frenzied flagellation. The cascade now rushes savagely down the path where only moments ago dry dirt and pebbles traced the way.

Inside, the family sits around the dinner table.

"Cy, I'm speaking to you," says Millie. At last he lifts his head from his book.

"Yes, dear?" and to his child, "Jeannie, why don't you eat your meal?"

"You're not listening to me, as usual I've been talking for ten minutes, you haven't heard a word I said."

"No, dear?" he said, bewildered. "I was thinking I'm glad it's raining, the cistern is a third empty."

"I said, Jeannie is getting too tall, she is already wearing size seven shoes and she is just eleven years old."

Jeannie looked up from her plate, interested; her mother continued with precise details.

"I heard there is a new method to control growth in children. Now listen to this. A surgeon in Houston, Texas, invented it: he saws off a piece of the thighbone—just an inch or two—for one thing the child gets shorter by that much, but the important thing is that the whole body stops growing. They call it 'discouraging growth.' Don't you think that it might be a good idea?"

The child asks, "What do they saw you with, Mommy, an electric saw or an old-fashioned one?"

"Not in front of her, dear," says Cy, his voice shaking.

"I don't know why not, this concerns her, I mean how is she going to find a husband if she is over six feet tall?"

Her concern was sincere; Millie herself had suffered so much because of her height. She knew men preferred little women. Cy looked at his child, already disgraced by braces and neglect, and wondered why it was that some women have the killer instinct in them. He tried to change the subject.

"Mrs. Goldfarb came back from her vacation this morning. She was tired from the flight, but she couldn't resist coming to the office all the same."

"I'm talking about Jeannie's big feet and you answer me with Mrs. Goldfarb," said Millie, outraged. "Can't you concentrate on what I'm saying?"

"Yes, yes—oh, I forgot to get your new sneakers—sorry, dear," he said to his child; "eat your carrots now," noticing that she was eating selected foods only, as usual.

The child knew how to take advantage of a situation.

"Can I go watch the Muppets, please, Daddy?"

"Right, but take your plate with you and finish it or else you will get it for breakfast," said Cy with an irritation he couldn't quite explain.

"Okay, I agree to the operation if I can have a motor-powered wheelchair, and," she added on her way to the living room, "I'll eat my carrots if you insist."

Cy plunged back into his book, defeated by the child's precocity, which he knew to be Millie's fault, hoping that now peace could be restored somehow.

"You think that you know what's best for that child," Millie said bitterly, "but just you wait until your darling stands six foot three in her loafers, we'll see who was right then," her voice rising to follow him as he stepped out to face the storm on the veranda.

He picked up a pot of cymbidiums tipped over by the wind; the crack in the pot annoyed him beyond reason, almost beyond endurance. He stood there, breathing deeply, allowing the turbulence of the night to take over, letting it blunt and temper his own violence. After a while he pushed all the pots forward to the edge of the veranda where they could receive the rain; he gave them as an offering to the storm, knowing that the rain would cleanse the dust and the gum from their leaves just as it was soothing the rage within his own heart.

The next morning, when the world was serene and innocent again, Millie walked out of the house, not knowing that the forest was once again a benign, smiling refuge to its inhabitants.

Cy heard the engine react painfully to her determined touch. He heard her try again, and sensed that she was offended that inanimate objects, too, should refuse to bend to her rational will; she tried again and again, while the engine only shook, retching with impotence; Cy was relieved when she gave up. Just as he expected, she stomped back, the screen door was ripped open, and now the plywood door, too.

"Cy, the engine's flooded," she yelled in the general direction of the bathroom. "I'm going to let you have my car—I'm taking your keys, dear."

She was already fastening the seat belt when she heard the screen door slap its aluminum frame. She screamed when she saw him. She just had time to think how white and vulnerable her husband's body was, and worse, how ridiculous his genitals looked bobbing up and down. She thought of a larva let out in the chrysalid stage. He was running toward her, his eyes in slits, his mouth set with determination, unconcerned by the main fact, the outstanding, the significant detail: that he was naked; she didn't utter a word, she only winced when he leaned over and grabbed the keys.

"No you don't!" he yelled with a passion more violent than she had ever seen in him. "No, you don't take my car—goddammit!" And with the keys safe in his clenched fist, he now calmly strolled off toward the house.

She sat in the car for a while, in a state of shock, trying to understand this new Cy she had just had a glimpse of.

After several suppositions, assumptions, most of which had to do with the fullness of the moon last night, the violence of the storm, and the undeniable deterioration of her husband's faculties—"Oh well, he's not getting any younger!" was his obituary—she finally exclaimed aloud, "That's it!" and in one instant eradicated fifteen years of doubts, sacrifices for some nonexistent common good, plump little lies fermenting with pus until now the abscess revealed itself to be the size of a cancer: "That's it and amen!" she repeated aloud and walked down the driveway and onto the road in the direction of her lawyer's office. All thoughts of Cy, the lover of her youthful days, were gone, banished from her thoughts now that her mind was preoccupied with the terms of her claim for indemnity against all those years of vexation.

Cy walked out of the house later than usual. This morning, however, he didn't go to his office, but instead followed the winding road that led up the mountain to a cluster of modest bungalows. The drive was so familiar that he did not need both hands on the wheel; through the open window of his blue Morris his right hand toyed with the fragrant breeze.

She came out of the house when she heard his car door slam. Still barefoot, still dressing, buttoning the white blouse over her full breasts, a soft smile curving her lips, dancing in her eyes, so that he thought to himself: How becoming white looks on her black skin; and once again, as every time he was near her, ever since he had met her at a school cocktail party that she, this full-bodied woman, had been invited to attend, he felt this surging, this surrendering of all his emotions, this animal contentment, so that in her presence he never wished for anything else but more and yet again more of her presence.

"My queen—my beautiful, darling woman—let's go inside, I want to hold you in my arms," he murmured lovingly as he let his hands slide down her back to her waist. The well-known curve of her hip fitted just right in the palm of his hand.

George Harcourt, Touring Actor

I have been married for thirty-five years. I am the star in the family. My wife is not even an actress, which might explain why she is bitter. She knows that she will leave no trace of herself after death, no one, not even our child, Evelyne, will murmur her name with a smile or tell a charming anecdote, recall something naïve, something kind or even outrageous she might have said or done. No, she will not even bequeath a cooking recipe to the world in memory of herself. She doesn't cook and doesn't care to. She gives the world just what she thinks it deserves. Nothing. No one can remember her calling a friend for a surprise "Happy Birthday, darling!" and she never says "Isn't this fun!" when given chopsticks to eat exotic fish in a tucked-away Japanese restaurant. She never caresses my arm to giggle coyly, "Lovely sweater you're wearing!" She never sighs with pleasure when the producer drives us in a stately white Rolls. She never, no she never . . . She takes all good things for granted and expects much more.

As soon as we arrived in this country, her sentence was

irrevocable: the prices are too high, the weather too cold, and its inhabitants too vulgar. The whole experience gives her one lasting migraine which will only leave her when she boards the plane for Los Angeles.

I, George Harcourt, her husband, sport a carefully controlled allure. Draped in the shreds of my worn-out fame, I keep a semblance of youth thanks to a trim haircut and a draconian diet. At sixty, my life has drifted into such a hopeless fiasco that I have to blot out reality in order to keep on living. For survival's sake I have become deaf to the vulgar sounds of day-to-day contingencies. In order to ensure that only the very essential sounds will reach my auditive faculties, or rather only the pleasant ones, I plug my ears to a Sony cassette machine from my waking hour onward, and, eyes piously closed, I listen to well-ordained classical music for some four to six hours running. Evelyne hardly comes to my mind. Evelyne, my daughter.

The evenings have to be sacrificed to the vulgar task of earning my living, and this is done with as much good grace as anyone can, who does not care to hear, see, or recognize any living being around him. After five weeks of daily contact, I truly do not know the name of the redheaded boy who calls the lights every night. After the same number of weeks I do not care to know the name of the actors who play with me. If I have to address one of them, I will call him or her by the name of the character he or she portrays. I never look anyone in the eye while talking. I don't want to get involved. Instead, I look immediately above their head or simply stare at an object as far away from their face as possible. Yes, it is true, I once talked to a fur coat hanging on the wall rather than to the actress who owned it.

Onstage I travel deaf and blind in an orbit of my own,

from which I will emerge only if sounds other than the usual ones jar my subconscious. On these occasions, my bewilderment is such that I need a minute or so and a lot of prompting from my partners before I can be brought back on the rails.

Needless to say, this self-imposed quarantine brings me excruciating boredom, but habit and my wife's perpetual discontent have imposed inflexible rules of aloofness from which I cannot depart.

Immediately after the show, impermeability to life is best maintained by soaking up red wine. A liberal ingurgitation of the stuff is desirable, though next day rigid abstinence will have to be observed, until after the show at least. My wife does not approve of these libations, so someone will be invited along to supper and the red wine ordered as if to please the guest. On these occasions I can be generous, but my wife, who is in charge of all financial affairs, grumbles. However, good food and wine being the only things I enjoy in the rarefied atmosphere we live in, I have decided to keep above such sordid matters. So, provided I am not disturbed in my thoughts or forced to partake in a conversation, I am pleased to foot the bill. I even enjoy presenting the image of a benefactor. Sometimes I reflect that there must be, deep down inside me, the atavistic residue of the joviality and generosity which are the heritage of men from the south. I could have been different, Evelyne could be with us now. Evelyne, my daughter.

You may think that I would seize the opportunity of those suppers to reminisce on the good old days or boast of past successes, shine with the easy tales of theatrical anecdotes, but no, I don't, my dinner guest will not be let off so easily. I have, I must admit, only one obsessional subject of conversation: that very night's attendance at the theater. Why was the auditorium not full? I suffer every empty seat as a personal affront, a burning wound to my pride, a thorn that cannot be removed from my flesh even with the anesthesia induced by a bottle of bordeaux. My chair askew so as not to face the table or the guest, I spend the best part of the supper in remote despair. My wife will tell me later that I am a bore and that if I will not enjoy the dinner, why pay for it? She says that she has already spent the best part of the day with a husband plugged to the spheres. In the evening, could I not spare her the torture of having to maintain the precariously thin conversation into which I blunder from time to time like a deaf man who pursues his inner monologue aloud? She says that every time I open my mouth the conversation collapses and she has to rebuild it from its foundations. My wife can be sarcastic.

When I look back, my career has been a series of little triumphs and bitter disappointments. As a young actor I smiled gratefully at my first public, but in later years my smile became a sour grimace. The world has forgotten my very existence and even those who remember have shelved me together with deposed kings, crippled race-car drivers, World War II heroes, and redundant politicians, only to be dusted and exhibited at the turn of a decade or on some such anniversary. "Twenty years ago in the movies . . ." will say the article. I live for those few moments when I can prove that I look almost as good as . . . then.

On this tour I am being exhibited with a partner of the same vintage as myself, because matrons like to see the idols of their courtship days.

The personnel around me, that is, my press agent, the stage manager, and my dresser, have to keep up the pretense of clamorous success and all the expressions of adulation must be sung in chorus before I can feel comfortable. Still, I feel frustrated. Just as a young child who is dominated by his parents, his elder brothers and sisters, the cook, and the dog too, asserts his ego over the only animal smaller than himself, the cat whom he tyrannizes, so I, George Harcourt, have to lord it over my dresser.

Every night, Art inquires with sincere concern as to my health, both mental and physical. My answer is curt if I feel well enough but have other worries on my mind, and lengthy when my little miseries need consideration. The problem is then analyzed and commented upon until satisfactory conclusions can be reached. My need for flattery is thus gratified. Certainly no one else in the company is ready to provide this service, particularly not my wife, who is not in an indulgent frame of mind after a perfectly empty day in her rooms. Of course, any sign of good humor or desire for reciprocity on the part of Art is discouraged. "It's time to get ready" will bring things back into their proper perspective.

When I am nearly ready I ask Art to wait for me at the entrance of the stage and to hold deferentially my hat and cane. The pretext is that I am forgetful, but Art instinctively knows that to stand at attention when I walk past him will please me, and indeed, I experience real glory for these seconds when I am served like royalty. The illusion is so quickly dissipated.

There is no doubt that my wife and I feel superior, so we feel entitled to impose endless little tasks on Art, who fulfills them with submissive patience. Every night, at curtain rise, my wife sits in the auditorium, her eagle eye picking on the smallest detail. She rushes backstage as soon as I have finished my first scene and orders more hooks and eyes to be sewn on my costume in order to keep the unwanted paunch from bulging. The flap that covers my zipper has to be firmly snapped down, and the waistcoat must be held to the trousers. Of course, all these little devices will snap off and unhook at the least movement, so that the spectator wonders what those bits of metal are, shining like war medals all over my person. But my wife knows best. Without her constant supervision I sometimes forget to zip up my trousers, so that more effort and thought have to be extended about my appearance than about my performance. Onstage, I feel as if a needle is stuck in the groove of an old record. I repeat the words on exactly the same tone every night.

Later, after the endless rectifications have been carried out, all part of the ritual to test Art's devotion, of course, I will request the ultimate service from him: wash up after me. Rather than use the general lavatory and be seen in the corridor, which might entail an exchange of pleasantries with other members of the cast, once or twice every night I relieve my bladder in my washbasin. I have no shame in doing this in front of Art or my wife. Coming from me, even unpleasant odors must be accepted. However, my wife refuses to wash the sink and I wouldn't know how to, and besides, there is a secret pleasure in asking Art to do the dirty work. Art receives a special bonus from the producer since he remarked that it was more in the line of a nurse's duty than of a dresser's.

As soon as the curtain goes up I send Art to fetch the stage manager to ask him what the takings are for the evening. If the takings are bad, I will vent bitter sarcasm against the spectators and blame my partners. If the house is full, something like a spark of joy will animate me. A skip and a jump quickly suppressed and a performance slightly less automatic are the only indications that I am pleased. But I still do not talk to anyone.

Last night, entering the theater at the last minute, just half an hour before curtain time, I was met at the stage door by Art and the stage manager. They seemed to be waiting for me because they stopped talking when they saw me. The compassionate tilt of their heads as they stepped forward to greet me told me immediately that something had happened. I shuddered, thinking of my daughter, and saw death in its frozen form. "Oh, Evelyne, Evelyne, the most beautiful flower on the Beverly Hills." I saw Evelyne, my child, sitting on my shoulders while I, her proud father, waded through the shallow end of the swimming pool. Holding my chin with moist little summer hands, Evelyne laughing self-consciously for the photographers. "He's so proud of her," said the press agent. And again, Evelyne the teenager, before that evanescent look changed her gaze, watching me flip the *crêpes bretonnes*, my French dexterity so appreciated by the photographers. But little by little, quiescence, indifference, took hold of Evelyne until one midday I found my daughter, seventeen, shut up in the den while the sun shone outside beckoning her to life in vain, staring in deep concentration at the gray flickers peppering the TV set. She had grown slovenly and listless and her face had taken on that puffy look while circles had sunken her eyes. I was made to understand by the doctor that she was under the influence of some profound hypnotic drug. The clinic said that it would take two years, three perhaps. How many times would she attempt suicide? How many times would she be saved? Was this the final one? How did she do it this time? Overdose? The razor? The window, when they weren't watching? My eyes begged to be spared the truth until after the show at least.

"Evelyne?" I uttered pitiably.

"What?" asked the manager, slightly off-balance.

Art was hiding something behind his back. The sentence—a newspaper. "In the papers already?" I murmured, frowning.

"Monsieur Harcourt . . . we've tried to find you and Madame Harcourt . . . your manager called from Hollywood. . . ."

I thought of my wife, so jealous of Evelyne's seventeen-year-old beauty. She'll never forgive me now. Oh, God, how shall I tell her?

"Yes? Well?" I insisted.

"Monsieur Harcourt, I'm very sorry to be the one to give you the bad news, but your Hollywood home was robbed last night."

"Robbed? What do you mean?" I couldn't comprehend why they would involve my home with Evelyne's death. She didn't live there anymore.

"Your secretary, sir. She was called by your neighbors. It seems they saw a truck move away at about 8 P.M. They looked through the windows because they knew that you were on tour and that your secretary was usually gone at that hour. They saw that everything was upside down in the house and there was yellow paint smeared everywhere—on the walls, the carpets, everywhere—a real desecration. . . ."

"Why are you holding this newspaper behind your back, Art?" I asked, still not convinced that Evelyne was not implicated in some terrible news.

"There's an article, sir, in the Rona Barrett column, with a picture of you."

"Let's see," I said, putting on my glasses. I read aloud: "HOME ROBBED AND VANDALIZED WHILE MATINEE IDOL ON TOUR." My eyes wandered toward the picture of myself.

"Hm . . ." I grunted. My shoulders straightened imperceptibly and my face lit up, suffused with the liberality I feel from time to time toward my dresser.

"Hm . . . I wonder where they got that picture. Quite good." I turned toward the manager.

"I'll get you a copy of it. I want you to pin it in the lobby, please. I think it's quite good of me."

Suddenly I remembered:

"Did you say yellow paint?"

Charles-Henri

When he was little and you asked him his name he would reward you proudly with: "Charles-Henri-sweetheart, three years old, acrobat."

A sepia photograph shows him, age seven, kilted like a little Scottish lord, slightly bow-legged in his patent leather pumps, a frown of suspicion on his brow, lending a reluctant hand to a mother of regal bearing. On one side the Mediterranean sea spreads its liquid body with serenity; on the other, palm trees in a receding line dot the sidewalk with their extravagant pompons. La Promenade des Anglais is perfectly recognizable and Charles-Henri and his mother seem whalebone-corseted against want and even against the possibility of scandal.

Charles-Henri was always Eglantine's favorite, the fact was revealed with unfair partialities; perhaps because he was the only boy and also the last born, but most probably because of the perfect beauty of his features: his blue eyes were dreamily fringed with long black lashes, his raven hair had just the right undisciplined curl, so that his mother could never resist his whims. But secretly, his nose was the feature she was most proud of; not a Garnier nose at all, authoritative, bony, beak-like, as was hers, but more like another she knew so well: a charming nose straight but not sharp, and not too long or too short either. His eyes, too, held infinite charm, with something slanted and caressing and yet an eager honesty, which made everyone say later that he was such a charming man. His sisters thought nothing of the difference in his looks, they were just a little jealous that all the admiring glances were for him. But then his charm encouraged them to cuddle him, dress him up in Mama's vaporous hats, the prettiest doll they had.

Charles-Henri lost his natural rebellion as a result of those games, his sisters dominating him with their stronger authority, which left a permanent weakness in his character when it came to women. He had a passion for his stamp collection, but the girls seldom allowed him to bring out his album, rather wanted him to play "baby in the buggy" or "doctor's visit" or again "tea with the King and Queen."

The façade of the Parisian mansion was so perfect that you had to wonder what shameful spot was rubbed off every morning on the brass door handle; twice a week the gardener combed the pebbles in Japanese waves, while the fountain gurgled soothingly for the goldfish, their silky flounces displayed with more grace than Isadora's.

The butler knew just the right respectful tilt of the torso when he opened the heavy front door at five-fifteen every day to Monsieur Guy Lepage, godfather of little Charles-Henri. And later, his white gloves were immaculate when he served tea for three, because although she couldn't help her boy with his homework as dear Guy could, Eglantine as often as possible would be present in the library while his godfather revealed the secrets of mathematics and Latin to Charles-Henri. In tacit accord, Guy and Eglantine, dainty tea sipped to the leaves, would retire and leave Charles-Henri to ponder and digest the tea cakes as well as the lessons.

As his mother's room was the next one, separated from the library by double doors, with only a little yard of corridor between them, voices would reach him in dimmed ripples of gaiety, or something like low velvety cooings and sighings, and again sometimes he would hear nothing at all. He would listen to those long silences, punctuated at every quarter by the crystal bell of a Napoleon III clock, pride of his father. There were orders in the household not to disturb those two hours of study. The girls were to stay upstairs in the nursery with Mademoiselle, while the servants had formal interdiction to come in, unless rung for. Later a chair was moved, a door opened, then the swish of Eglantine's petticoats brushing against furniture and suddenly the brilliancy of voices would burst into the room, while perfume emanating from her own delicate skin, it seemed, enveloped her exquisitely feminine presence with charm and mystery.

Everyone agreed that Eglantine was the most enchanting woman, a bird, a flower, fine and pliant as a reed, while her bearing was prouder than any queen's. That was why her husband never hesitated to add another gold chain or strand of pearls to her incomparable neck.

At a quarter to seven, Guy Lepage would put on his chamois gloves and, having kissed his pupil with enough affection to last him until tomorrow, would descend the staircase preceded by la Belle Eglantine, who always saw him to the door.

Marcel Garnier never came home before seven-thirty, so that he and Guy Lepage never crossed paths in the house. And although Guy Lepage came to tea every day and was the accountant for all of Marcel Garnier's affairs, he was never invited to dinner and never asked to those wonderful weekends in the house at Vaux-sur-Seine, outside Paris. There were never any answers as to why this was so, and if a child persisted in asking questions, his father would remind him sharply that it was indiscreet to meddle in grown-up affairs. The subject was closed and quite obviously the next violation of decorum and tact would send you up to your room.

In his bed at night before drifting into sleep Charles-Henri often wondered about this adult mystery as well as this other one: why did his godfather have the same name as these bunches of mistletoe, called *gui* in French, which he could see growing in the trees on the little island in front of the house? What had his gentle, slanted-eyed godfather to do with mistletoe? He never voiced the question, so he never received an answer.

Charles-Henri's father adored his girls, loved to sit one flounced girlie on each knee and kiss their necks until they giggled because his beard tickled them. Papa was weak and lovable, hated it when anyone quarreled, which is unusual in a lawyer, and he simply capitulated when Eglantine would bar the door of her bedroom to obtain a new pony or a pond for the country estate, or a winter garden to englass her chilly orchids. But with Charles-Henri, Marcel Garnier was different. He was lenient and generous but more with a sense of duty, kind but polite, a little distant, too, as if he had no rights over this son of his. Marcel Garnier was always aware that he must be fair with this child as well.

There were hushed words and gossiping behind the pantry door, though. One afternoon after his godfather had left, Charles-Henri was sitting on the kitchen floor hugging his knees while Alban, the butler, played the accordion for him, and before she opened the glass door or saw him sitting there, Odilia, Alban's wife, cried out to her husband, "Had to change her sheets again. Why can't they think of me when they hump?" And she came through the door, her arms loaded with sheets so that she couldn't see him sitting so still on the kitchen floor. In the ensuing silence, while the accordion died with a sigh, its pleated lungs deflated, Charles-Henri heard the echo over and over in his head, as rings form in the water when you throw a stone, form and reform the same pattern, endlessly; he heard, endlessly, "When they hump—when they hump—hump—hump—hump."

One Sunday afternoon the incident took place that caused a permanent change in Charles-Henri's life. While they were strolling in the Bois de Boulogne, all five of them, Marcel and Eglantine arm in arm, while Charles-Henri was running circles around his parents, trying to catch the girls, suddenly there appeared in front of them Guy Lepage and a charming-looking lady, who was leaning on his arm in the most feminine way. Although she said not a word, only caught her breath, Charles-Henri was aware that his mother had received a great shock. Introductions were made, a few banalities exchanged while the couples recovered their composure. Eglantine, for no reason at all, was out of breath when they parted.

Later at home she went straight to bed, complaining of an excruciating headache. There was a great deal of agitation throughout the house, with Odilia running out of Mama's room holding a basin full of bloodied towels, the doctor rushed in urgently while Charles-Henri, who had been told nothing, cried, thinking that his mother was dying of some sudden illness or accident. "Only a nosebleed, sweetheart; one way of getting it out of her system! Don't worry, she won't die of it, there's a good boy. . . ." Odilia running down the stairs with her armload of bloodstained rags, which had a sticky sweet odor to them, stopped a minute to take him in her arms and console him for the last great sorrow of his childhood.

Guy Lepage never came back to help Charles-Henri with his homework, and the dear boy was sent away to the most exclusive boarding school in France.

They called him Charlie there. He wore his cap at a rakish angle and his stockings rumpled over his boots. He rode his bicycle into town, first to raid the local pastry shop, later to go to the movies where he saw newsreels of the war to end all wars, and later still for his initiation into the town whorehouse. Altogether Charlie spent ten years learning to be the perfect French gentleman.

In 1930, aged twenty-two, while he was going through the tedious business of learning law, he met a honey of a girl. Bleached blond, she had been on the stage, yes even on Broadway, and admitted it unashamedly. Somehow the fact that she was American, had been married, was now a divorcée and also six years his senior, made her all the more desirable. His sisters and mother said, "A little fast, isn't she?" when they saw the bright colors she wore and the cigarette between her fingers, but Charlie decided to marry this fascinating woman who knew what was what and had many secrets in her past.

Everyone agreed that the wedding in the church of La Madeleine was a glorious success and the bride a perfect Botticelli.

Cora was her name, and soon the shady spots in her past became clear to Charlie, who wished he could rub them off as easily as the stains on the brass handle of his front door. He really preferred not to know, though at night he couldn't help recalling what Cora had said about the difficulties of surviving in New York on just a dancer's pay, and also something about the boredom of having to be "nice" to men if you wanted them to pay for dinners and things. She was fond of describing, with roars of laughter that didn't go down well at all with his kind of people, how she had shared a dressing room with a Japanese mime and learned the secrets of his shaving every single hair on his body. No doubt his sister was right, Cora drank too much at dinner, and right again, he suspected, when she said that there was something of the gold digger in Cora but that she only succeeded in being brassy.

But Cora came into her own when they were alone in the bedroom. She was so provocative in her carelessness, almost innocent in her sluttish abandon. Like a showgirl who stands backstage unaware of her nudity, she would walk around in the scantiest underwear, and Charlie was particularly aroused by her collection of garter belts, straps held together with the minimum of black lace, to uplift, bind, but mostly reveal. The crudeness of her language in the sexual games she liked to play would have been shocking had it not been for her foreign accent, which in fact spiced things up.

Charlie knew he was endangering his career; he realized it each time his wife made a faux pas at the formal dinners they attended, and no doubt it was because of his marriage that he was not getting important cases to defend. He wondered about himself. Why had he, who had been raised by the most exquisite of mothers, chosen a woman so inferior to the Garnier women? Why did he feel the need to be degraded? He despised Cora's vulgarity and yet was her pupil, let her dominate him.

This ambivalence caused him pain, made him hesitant and tentative; Cora noticed that even his sneezes were subdued now.

He would say nothing to her, did not advise her on proper behavior or try to stop her, for instance when she wanted to wear that mauve satin dress which he hated. He changed his behavior rather than let her notice she was out of step. Once in a while, though, Charlie took refuge in his mother's salon, where he went alone now, because Cora felt that the discreet atmosphere was a crashing bore and also because she had quarreled with Charlie's elder sister over some sarcastic remarks she had made.

Cora, in her own circle, exulted. She bedecked herself in the Garnier prestige with the ostentation of a peacock, boasted about their wealth, and was slightly irritated by the raised eyebrows of those for whom extravagance is not a delight but a tiresome obligation.

But she was no fool. Although she could not resist the pleasure of wearing Grandmother Garnier's diamond in broad daylight, a slipup if ever there was one, she was well aware of what was going on during those family evenings, when Charlie pretended tactfully that his father wanted to discuss business with him and she would say that she wasn't feeling well, but might later drop in at a friend's for coffee and girls' talk. She knew there would be subtly derisive comments made about her, met with half smiles and sniggers. She could feel by his reticence, when she would question him later, that his family had done their best to undermine his love for her. She responded in her own way. In that world where so many marriages are a business move for power, position, or money, there is no shortage of men eager for a good time. And let's face it, the idea of taking down the Garnier swank was part of the fun. So Cora picked herself a lover, and when she got tired of him she changed, changed often, in fact.

Charlie knew and yet did not look for proof, minded and yet did nothing. First he was surprised that anyone could treat him this way, then it became annoying, really annoying, to be made a fool of, and then it turned into a pain that was almost sweet in its intensity. Can it make sense to say that he was in a way relieved to know that other men appreciated his wife and that the torment of jealousy was almost as fulfilling as love itself? Finally Charlie convinced himself that these things were inevitable; therefore he accepted them.

The great cataclysm, World War II, brought an end to their union. The more imminent the news, the more restless Cora became. She was, it must be said, disappointed in her husband's career, having expected much quicker advancement in society and larger figures in their bank statements. Charlie would say, "Please be patient, it takes time to build a clientele." She would shrug her shoulders and give it to him straight: "In the States we say that if you haven't made your first million by thirty, you're never going to make it, buddy!"

Around the spring of 1939 Cora, who had a good sense of timing, started sending crates to New York, discreetly, without Charlie's knowing it. Just a few good things, silver candlesticks, dishes, some Lalique glasses, their best linen. She was ready for her getaway.

She waited to see how things turned out, waited till war was declared and the Germans finally started to advance through Belgium into France, waited until almost too late, in fact. Charlie was away on the fast-retreating front, assigned to supply duties, when she hastily packed all her garb, not forgetting furs, hats, gloves, shoes, umbrellas, and even bits of fabric left over by the dressmaker. She had booked her berth on the last boat leaving from Le Havre. Charlie, just before going to sleep in a ditch somewhere north of Paris, read this sweet but short letter:

"Darling, I'm off to New York for a while. I feel this is the wrong time to be a foreigner in Paree. Your family would certainly not lift a finger for me in case of trouble and who knows if you'll be around. . . . (Sorry to be so frank.) But remember I'm not abandoning you, just being cautious, which you certainly want me to be. Let's meet at the Ritz when this stupid war is over. Loads of love from your Cora."

Soon after, Lieutenant Charles-Henri was wounded while still in uniform. Not that he was hit by any bellicose weapon, but his left arm was broken when a truckful of homing pigeons, who had had no chance to serve in this short war either, overturned, pinning him and his stolen bicycle under a pile of feathery cages. He felt himself a failure even in his war efforts, but plowed on for the next four and a half years, trying to find fresh butter for his mother's delicate stomach and to get in touch with Cora, which proved impossible.

The war ended in quite a different world. The Garnier fortune was no more, Marcel Garnier's probity having been questioned in the shady transactions of a department store of which he was major shareholder and president. The result was irreversible ruin. Monsieur Garnier was asked to resign from his multiple activities and sell all his shares at what proved to be a disastrous rate. The house in Neuilly and the one in the South of France were hastily sold, the weekend retreat practically stolen by ruthless lawyers.

The loss of fortune and position was too great a shock for Eglantine. She longed so earnestly for an illness to take the tangible form of her despair that an all too real cancer took hold of her willing flesh. She gave her soul to God on a cold Sunday morning in February.

Warm shoes were scarce in those days; perhaps that was why fewer friends than had ever been to her Wednesday luncheons accompanied her to the grave. Her three children were there, of course, holding, buoying up Marcel Garnier, an old man now. The leaden sky and thinly, softly falling snow played tricks with Charlie's eyes. The voice of the priest was muted; more real was the steam coming out of his mouth. The black and white lunar bareness of these last rites made Charlie weep for past joys and laughter. It was at that moment, when all stepped forward to witness with dread the casket being lowered into the frozen hole, that Charlie saw, or thought he saw, thought he recognized at a distance, across the grave, the slight figure half hidden behind a tree. She was staring at him, too, then nodded, and that rosebud mouth of hers sketched a fugitive smile. That brave provocative smile, still able to create the effect of winning—of winning what? Oh yes, he remembered. They all came back to him, the countless petty victories over unsuspecting foes, engaged in small battles she alone kept the score of. And always that smile, to hide the susceptibility of a girl born on the wrong side of the tracks, who would not for the world let you know where the shoe pinches. Yes, Cora was back.

Her wardrobe was a little shabby, her French had become rusty, and her manner was changed. Although she didn't go into details, she admitted having gone through

rough times and was grateful for a rest. She wasn't as forthright and assertive as she used to be, but took a few seconds before answering, not only because the right word didn't come easily, but as if she were following a mental blueprint.

Charlie was reminded of their first encounter when she displayed her wit with a thousand insidious tricks. "To what end? Why is she trying so hard to please me?" Charlie did not understand her motives. Of course, there had been the separation of the war, painful for him; times full of doubts about the validity of his privileged position now that the family wealth was frittered away to nothing, doubts about his adequacy as a husband and mostly about her return. He was frankly surprised to see her back, but relieved and grateful to see she still retained her magic spell over him.

Charlie and Cora settled in an apartment where very little remained of past splendors. The creaking floorboards in the corridor were not replaced and the kitchen tiles, where wood had been chopped during the war, were left unsealed and broken. Cora used her imagination only in the drawing room, where she displayed unfashionable Victorian furniture covered in white moiré. She was surprised when Charlie mentioned rather tentatively that the effect was a little chilly. He thought, with a quick pinch of the heart, that all this icy whiteness revealed her inability to love him. Why had she never wanted children, for instance? These were thoughts he chased away from his mind as unworthy of her and of himself, for that matter. Still, he would have preferred vast soft armchairs and warm colors to this rigid pretension.

When the apartment was finished, he felt a pause within

Cora, a moment of satisfaction, a preening of the feathers, a licking of the paws before planning the next move, whatever it was going to be. Charlie waited. He felt the inevitable brink coming close, toward which their marriage was progressing, the revelation, the unmasking of its lunacy or hoax.

Cora told him innocently about the arrival of her cousin Stan "from New York. He'll be here for a while. Do you mind if we have him to dinner? He's very nice."

In fact, Charlie thought that Stanley Gilbert was rather vulgar. There was something smooth about him that was distasteful. He had an irritating if friendly way of touching your arm when he spoke, to make sure you were listening or that you had understood him. Dressed in garish clothes, red socks, a red sweater even, he wore a belt that was far too wide to be fashionable. Charlie was reminded of the belts acrobats wear, with the hook on the side into which the teacher snaps a rope to hold the pupil, while practicing somersaults. Or again, of the waist pinchers that vain gentlemen wore in his father's day, to hold in an unsightly paunch; what's more, Stan's fingers were too preciously manicured, reflected Charlie. But these were only details. What Charlie minded was that Stan Gilbert did not play the game with gentlemanly fairness. He seemed not only in control of himself, but to be manipulating others as well; he didn't want you probing too closely into his affairs or motives, yet was most inquisitive about the family situation and other delicate matters. But to the question "What are your plans while in Paris?" he would look quizzical and give you some shaggy-dog story, the most sensible version being that he was here to write a series of articles on Europe for *National Geographic*.

He was, in fact, often at the house and usually before Charlie came home from his office. The first time Charlie saw him in the library, lounging in his own armchair, Cora, who never did this, had rushed to greet him at the door, so sweet and eager that Charlie thought it strange. "I was so lonely this afternoon, Stan came to have tea with me." A faint echo reverberated from some long-forgotten memory, a shame or a betrayal he had lived once before and suffered through. That evening Charlie felt embarrassed in front of his wife's cousin, as if he had failed in some task he was meant to accomplish.

Charlie woke up during the night, something hot and sticky blocking his nose, impeding his breathing. He got up from bed, tottered unstably in front of the bathroom mirror to stare, aghast, at his bloodied face. Streaks of the dark red stuff had run down his cheeks from his bleeding nose, caking his ears and hair. He called Cora, who helped him back to bed, sponged the blood while murmuring soothing words until it stopped bleeding and he could go back to sleep. He woke up with a headache and a fever, but went to the office just the same. At one o'clock he felt so ill that he came home and went to bed. The doctor was called, who ordered aspirin and rest. Later Cora introduced Stan, who had come to inquire about his health. That evening the fever was so high that the doctor was called again. This time he diagnosed pneumonia and suggested that Charlie be transported to the hospital. But Charlie refused categorically, so Cora had to take care of him as best she could.

He slept through phantasms and hallucinations, his worst fear being that Cora, this bird on the tree, the threatening tree itself, then the tiger at the end of the bed and the balloon they were bringing close to his face, Cora, his precious wife, was leaving, leaving again. The illness lasted twelve days, during which Cora oscillated between concern and impatience. The phone rang often for her and she answered sometimes in the sickroom, with sighs and endless, hushed murmurs. She went out every day. "I can't stand being cooped up like this," she said upon her return, her gay mood lifting him out of his torpor. "Stan took me to the movies. I was so depressed, always at home. Are you better?"

Charlie was a long time getting better, probably because he knew he had lost his battle against the odds of life.

It happened early in the morning, after what seemed to Charlie endless days and nights alone in that small bed, Cora having moved him to the guest room at the beginning of his illness. "It can't be more than eight-thirty," he reflected, the fever madness being now only intermittent. Only eight-thirty, yet he was sure that the voices were hers and Stan's. They were quarreling with the intimacy of two people who have rights over each other. He couldn't catch what Stan said because his voice was more controlled, lower. But Cora, screaming: "I'm sick and tired of your demands. Seems to me you're doing mighty fine, considering. Just watch out I don't take off for Mexico. . . ." The rest of the sentence was blurred by the door of his room opening and the maid bringing his breakfast on a tray. "Tell me, Blanche, is Monsieur Gilbert in the house?" The maid looked guilty, was silent for a few seconds before answering, her eyes lowered to the tray. "I don't know, monsieur, shall I ask Madame?" "No, no. If he's here I'll probably see him in a minute." He lay still on his pillow while his imagination leaped forward and disclosed to his perception the equation that took form, shape, and from illusion became substance. Cautiously, with infinite pains, he pulled himself out of his bed, strengthened by the certainty, unshakable as if he had already seen the official seal stamped at the bottom, with the notary's signature and the names, Cora Stoddard and Stanley Gilbert, and the date and place, the marriage certificate folded in three, locked up in Cora's desk, with the key hidden away in the pencil jar. When he found the official form, pompous and banal as a Mexican restaurant menu, he realized he had seen it many times with his mind's eye.

How often had he retraced her steps? Cora arriving in New York, with a name that couldn't help her there, a French name that meant nothing to that crowd—her francs worth very little—then her diamond sold and the rest too, little by little, and then what? Encounters, certainly—such a beautiful woman—but maybe bad luck, too—who was there to take care of little Cora? She was not true sterling anyway, or so she thought. Better go back to ballet, her world—had given ballet classes then, or done a nightclub act with Stan Gilbert—that acrobat's belt, yes—the team, Cora and Stanley—love? Affinity rather, or protection—his authority over her—the master, which he, Charlie Garnier was not. . . . The ballet master. . . . And where? tours—after the big city, small towns, summer spots—Atlantic City, Tulsa, Phoenix, Santa Fe, and from there, Mexico—and why not? The temptation to say yes to the quick divorce and marriage . . . this never-ending war . . . Paris, so far away now.

Charles-Henri could only sit on the floor, his arms hugging his knees, while he recalled the tune Alban was playing on his accordion, that afternoon many years ago:

"When they hump–when they hump–hump–hump–hump." Charlie cried out, "Godfather!" and Guy Lepage came in, bent over him, looking at him with his gentle slanted eyes. "Why me? Why did this happen to me? Did you do this to me, Father?"

Vengeance

Standing on the kitchen table, she stares at her naked body mirrored in the blind windowpanes; the shadows of night lingering under the eucalyptus tree in this tardy dawn serve as a reflector.

"My name is Malison—I'm your souvenir of 1957. . . ."

Malison has hardly slept, she had to get ready; she has now washed herself all over in the metal basin, right on the old red tile floor (in water heated on the stove with wood from the pile outside the door), washed her long hair and aired it to dry in front of the oven door, brushed her nails, hands, and feet with the kitchen scrubbing brush, cleaned her ears with a corner of the long, fringed cotton towel wrapped around a match, and now stands appraising severely this body of hers. "Is it hard and lean, muscular enough for killing?" Yes, she is fine-boned and sinewy; hers is a life-force, an organism used to speed and skill rather than muscular strength; she will kill him fast.

As a young girl she was already the champion of her

mother's honor. They called her "Malison, the little lion." At the first provocation she would attack and rout the foe.

"When I'm eighteen I'll come and kill you. . . ."

She has the will all right, and the decision was taken long ago when she first found out about the interlude that caused her mother's life to be wasted; and if she had at any time wavered in her decision or lost her single purpose, what happened on that Sunday a year ago would have reaffirmed her resolution to kill her father; she had always set the date for her eighteenth birthday, and this was the day. She will now dress quickly before anyone wakes up in the house, and set out to walk the ten miles to the town of S. Her feet will get swollen and sore, because she isn't used to walking long distances in shoes, but the hatred in her heart will make her forget the pain; she will do it running if need be; did she not walk nearly that distance, barefoot, every summer morning to work at ironing shirts at the laundry and pay for her studies?

"My name is Malison—I'm your souvenir of 1957. When I'm eighteen I'll revenge my mother."

At first she knew her only as "the lady," later as Graziella, and only much later as her mother. She was a little chit of a girl, three or four years old maybe, and at that time lived on another farm where she was made to sleep with the animals on dirty straw, when this lovely lady, who smelled of perfumed soap and wore a golden chain and cross around her neck, picked up the frightened little savage she had become, after seeing that she was covered in scabs and scratched herself like a flea-bitten mongrel, and, trying to disentangle the dirty matted hair with her fingers, murmured, "My poor child—my poor little girl—how I wish you could stay with me."

The lady had taken her away and brought her here to

this farm where she always had enough to eat and slept in a bed. Of course, Malison didn't really remember those early days. Later the descriptions of her first home as told by her mother took on such vivid colors in her imagination that she mistook Graziella's recollections for her own; but the cunning resilience of a homeless animal, her own strength, was seeded then; her fear of rejection remained.

Every year Graziella, the lovely sad lady, came to see her. She asked endless questions, wanted to know everything about little Malison. The child liked the visits, would stare hours on end from a corner of the kitchen at this lady with delicate plump hands who revealed a corner of her pale silky underwear when she lifted her skirt before sitting down. Malison felt a little embarrassed when it was time for the lady to leave, as she would embrace her passionately, with tears in her eyes, cover her face with kisses, and always murmur the same words: "My darling, darling little girl. How I wish you could stay with me."

After her departure Malison would run up to the room where the lady had slept, to smell with rapture the clean perfume that floated palpably in the air and also the tube of cream left behind for Malison to spread on her face in the mornings "before going out in the sun, to protect her fine skin," but which was soon forgotten in a kitchen drawer, or used on the cows' udders when they were chafed.

She was eight when she found out. It was a hot summer's afternoon, but the room was relatively cool because the shutters were closed, only admitting a streak of brilliancy, almost a neon strip across the soft penumbra.

Malison took off her dress to luxuriate in the sheets still impregnated with the lady's fresh scent, seduced by, dreaming of this world of niceties and solicitude she could perceive, where care of self comes before the tyranny of the soil and animals. Lulled away by the afternoon's torpor, the room shimmering and receding to the rhythm of the cicadas' monotonous lullaby, she was suddenly alerted that something else was there, another breath stirring the tranquil air, a threat, a presence usurping this privileged moment.

Nonchalantly, Nano revealed himself. Although there was plenty of teasing between them, she loved her brother, at least she thought of him as such.

"This is Graziella's room," she said with authority; "get out and leave me be!"

He jeered as boys will, "Listen, this is my home, not yours, and your mother is nothing but a whore."

"What do you mean, my mother is a whore? Our mother is not a whore," she replied indignantly.

"You're more of a baby than I thought," he said. "Don't you know who your mother is? You're just here as a lodger. That means that your mother pays us to keep you."

"Who is my mother, then?"

"Graziella, you dummy."

"Graziella is my mother?" she repeated, unbelieving. "Mama is not my real mother?"

She cried, not because she did not love Graziella enough to accept her as her mother, but because the order of things had been changed.

"You're a love child," said Nano, and not too sure of his terms, he added, "You're improper. Your father never married your mother."

"Why not? Who is he, who is my father?"

But Nano could not tell her, because he did not know.

Malison went to the woman she had thought of as her mother, but she did not know either; she had to wait for a whole year before Graziella's return in order to ask her. During that year she grew up fast, not in size, but in her perception of things. She realized that she had no more rights in this household than the cuckoo's egg hatched illegitimately, and that her mother had been paying for the affection she had up till now accepted as her birthright.

Graziella did not find it easy to disclose her secret; the reckoning of her disgrace haunted her still. She remembered vividly her secret confinement when she must hide by day and could leave her room only furtively by night, and how her father, who still had not forgiven her, had driven her far away to a hospital where the nuns let her scream for twenty-four hours without giving her anesthetics or anything to ease the pain, just because they knew that she was not married. Graziella could not say all this to her child, so she said that she remembered very little. This is all she told at first:

"When I was a young girl, I was sent to the town of S. to finish my studies. I stayed with an old aunt who let me come and go as I pleased. I knew very little of life, brought into the city straight from the convent."

Graziella told how she had been befriended by a young man, who was married, a teacher who had shown her around the museums, taken her for outings, a picnic by the river; after, she had gone to church every day and prayed. Time had passed and what she feared most had happened. When her father found out, because she couldn't hide it any longer, he became very angry and said she was an abomination and did not deserve to see the light of day. After she gave birth, he arranged for the nuns to give her baby away to a foster-mother in the country and paid this woman through the nuns, without even wanting to know who she was or where she lived, and so Graziella did not see her baby for three years. The woman was wicked, she had taken the money and practically let the baby die of neglect.

Malison kept questioning her mother until finally she pieced the story together. She realized that her mother's life had been destroyed by that man. He had condemned her to survive and bear her dishonor for the remaining years of her adulthood. Malison understood that the experience of giving birth in secrecy had marked her mother so deeply that she had abandoned her rights to love and share the life of another man; her heart had lost the first illusions of innocence, no young man she could meet would have had the store of experience she had, so she never married.

Graziella remained in her father's house as a housekeeper and took in some sewing; she was barely tolerated at home. The recollection of her "depravity" remained vivid in her father's mind, even after all these years. At first she cried a lot, but little by little she became more peaceful, forgot laughter and gaiety at the same time as she forgot despair. Her dormant emotions were revived only for a brief moment every year when she paid a visit to Malison, her child.

Malison realized that her destiny was extraordinary and felt a compulsion to do something heroic to match such a fate. She was twelve the first time she called her father on the telephone.

"My name is Malison. . . ."

"Who? Who is this?"

"I am Malison—your souvenir of 1957."

"What does this mean? Who are you?"

"I'm your souvenir of 1957, when I'm eighteen I'll avenge my mother. . . ."

"Your mother?"

"Graziella, my mother."

There was a silence, she could hear him breathe faster. She was sure that he was suddenly afraid or guilty.

"When I'm eighteen I'll find you and I'll KILL YOU!"

She hung up, but stayed, her hand on the phone, panting, trembling from head to foot, and then she started to think about the voice and the man who owned that voice. What was he like? She invented a silhouette, a shape, broad shoulders that wore the white shirt with grace, the jacket balanced on his shoulders on hot summer's evenings, and fine hands that held the cigarette casually. She saw him, thin dark curly hair slightly disheveled crowning a pale gaunt face, deep-set black eyes, so profoundly serious, intent with such longing, such hunger for Graziella's love that his voice would choke when he pleaded with her. Malison saw him everywhere, on the faces of saints in her missal, on the photographs in front of cinemas, inside the rowdy cafés of a Sunday afternoon; she even guessed at his image among the foliage when she peered through the dark window at dinnertime. But when she dreamed of him in her sleep he never had a face, or at least she couldn't remember it when she woke up.

She called him every year on her birthday. At first she tried to deepen her voice, to give it as much strength as she could. But there was no need anymore; every year her voice was stronger, more assertive, and more raucous, too, from yelling after the animals in the fields.

"My name is Malison–I'm your souvenir of 1957. Today is my eighteenth birthday. I'm coming to kill you."

She opened the wardrobe fully so that the drawer would have room to slide out. She knew just where the Luger was. There, under the pile of linen, wrapped inside Bartolo's old army shirt. Once, when he had drunk too much grappa, he had pulled it out of its hiding place and told the family how he had taken it from a dead German, how the body was still warm and limp when he had turned it over on its back and only then had he seen that it didn't have a face anymore. He had kept the gun out of some sort of respect for the poor bastard; even though dead is dead, he felt that in some way this defacement made it more tragic; perhaps because the corpse inspired horror rather than pity. That story had always haunted little Malison: the dead German soldier had become her father and she always thought that she would do just that to him, deface him, cover with blood the face that had seduced her mother.

She knew that the gun was well oiled. She checked the magazine. It was all right. Now she wrapped it up again in the old shirt, put it in the bottom of the big soft straw basket she used to carry things.

Before leaving the kitchen, she cut herself a large slice of bread and sprinkled some sugar on it. She was hungry.

Walking toward town, she tried not to think of Franco, but nearly every turn of the road reminded her of him. Already a year since their last night together and she still felt something soft and mellow when his name came up in her mind, though she would not let herself pine for him. Despite herself she remembered the way he had of walking with her on this road, springing up and down, forehead forward, his eyes shining, so alive with projects for their life together. No, she couldn't allow herself to think about him, those tender feelings were burned out by what had happened that Sunday a year ago. How many times had she relived the encounter with his mother, when, coming out of church, Malison had walked smiling toward Franco and his mother had stopped her by the shoulder and shoved her aside while she went on walking down the steps holding her son by the arm, guiding him away from Malison, and then turned back and shouted loud enough for the whole village to hear her: "Keep away from my son, *puttana!* You are nothing but the daughter of a whore! My son is not for you!" She had repeated louder still, "*Puttana!*"

People had passed Malison, pursing their lips as if she were a dead animal rotting in the gutter, fouling the air.

She had not gone to church since or spoken to him, although he had tried to contact her. No, she could never see him again, or speak to him, let alone be touched by him.

She kept on walking with her decisive stride, swinging her arms freely, past the olive groves, past the vineyards, past the orchards. She knew that death stood at the end of the road, grinning at her. Now the first gas station appeared, announcing the town, the first *palazzini*, still unfinished but festooned already with drying sheets and greenery; the first fruit and vegetable shop and the butcher shop exhibiting a brace of rabbits, frozen by death in their last leap.

She knew where she was going. She entered the hotel and asked for the telephone in a firm voice. The concierge pointed to the booth. It was not quite nine o'clock.

"*Pronto,*" he answered.

"I am Malison—your souvenir of 1957. Today is my

eighteenth birthday—I have come to kill you. I am waiting at the Hotel Splendid—now." She could sense him thinking up evasive excuses, subterfuges. "If you don't come right away I'll go to your house and tell your wife."

He sighed deeply and said, "All right, I'll be there in half an hour."

She hung up without saying another word. She knew she would recognize him straight away. Forty-three—forty-five, he must have some gray hair mixed with the black. The hairline must have receded a little, extending his forehead, deepening his eyes. His fine face must be thinner, more like a bird's than when he was young. She knew that when she aged she would look like a bird too. "I will look like him," she had always thought. And again, "He may wear glasses—he reads so much."

She went to the ladies' room to cool her feet in the bidet of one of the toilets. She came back into the lobby and positioned herself in an armchair facing the entrance. Her heart was beating violently. She had to take deep breaths, she seemed to have lost the knack of breathing.

A couple drifted down, obviously American tourists. She looked away, dismissing them from her mind. Presently a busload came in through the revolving doors, which were then fixed in the open position. The bellboys got very busy with their carts loading mountains of luggage. With unseeing eyes she followed the group massed at the desk; her mind was fixed on her purpose. She didn't pay much attention to the paunchy, balding man, a straggler from the group no doubt, who settled his flabby shape in an armchair on the other side of the coffee table. She kept looking at the door where her father would come in.

The couples were going up noisily to their rooms, disturbing her concentration. She was annoyed that the middle-aged man seemed in no hurry to go up with the others. She looked at his face; he seemed to ooze heat from every pore. He looked at his watch impatiently. With a handkerchief he wiped the folds of his baggy face. Observing the drooping curve of his narrow shoulders, she remarked inwardly how commonplace the middle-aged Italian man was. She wished this man would go and leave the lobby free for the confrontation that was to take place. She waited nervously, staring at the door. The man waited too.

It only dawned on her slowly that this man . . . "Oh no! Not possible! This man my father? No, this ordinary man cannot be my father—he mustn't be my father." A great sweep of nausea churned her stomach.

She could imagine the routine banality of his life: the vain parade in front of his colleagues at work while at home a whimpering despot; his boring conversations at the table, the sluggish digestion after the overindulgent meals. She was revolted by the mediocrity she sensed in that soft, pear-shaped body.

She stared at him hard, unblinking, a severe frown splitting her forehead. Conscious of the bold gaze, his eyes, although looking in the direction of the entrance, were called to look at hers, at this minute, slim young girl, with a face alert and delicate like a bird's, buried in the armchair opposite the round table, her brown wavy hair spread like a silky shawl over her thin shoulders.

They stared for a while across the round table, the air charged with emotion.

She spoke first; he recognized at once the raucous voice: "I am Malison."

He nodded, surprised that this exquisite little porcelain figurine should be his executioner. He blinked away the perspiration that had accumulated in his wrinkled eyelids.

Finally he took out the handkerchief again and tried to sponge dry his turgid flesh held together by wrinkles where perspiration collected, only to run down to the next swelling of skin.

"I am Malison," she repeated, "Graziella's daughter." She felt like shouting at him, "Stand up like a man so that I can shoot you!"

He tried to compose a pleasant expression on his face. "Malison, *ciao, cara,* you are so pretty–"

"No compliments, please. I'm here to kill you," she said harshly.

He looked nervously around and then down at her large basket and understood that she had a weapon in there. Her eyes confirmed it.

"All those years," he said tentatively, "and we didn't meet. Such a lovely girl . . . Where do you live?" Malison looked at him sternly, not answering. "And your mother? How is she? She . . . she was such a lovely girl . . . impetuous, of course . . . and passionate. She didn't tell me, you see . . ." said he lamely.

"My mother's life is ruined. You ruined my mother's life. My mother never married–her life was over before it ever began, all because of you. My mother was locked up in her room during her pregnancy. A young girl locked up for four months–the food was brought up to her in her room–twice a day she was allowed to the bathroom to wash–she had pains–she was frightened about what was happening to her–she cried but no one came. They refused to give her anesthetic at the hospital because she was not married–she screamed with pain for twenty-four hours–where were you during all that time?"

She was panting with anger stored up for so long. He

looked around, noticed that the employees at the desk were staring at him with interest. He gave an embarrassed smile.

"Ssh! Not so loud . . . I didn't know . . . She didn't tell me . . . We stopped seeing each other," he said meekly.

"Didn't you even call to know how she was? You did, didn't you? And she told you, didn't she?" Her eyes were burning with outrage.

"Yes . . . yes . . . that is true. It is so long ago, I forget. You mustn't be angry with me. We must be friends."

"Friends! You ruined my mother's life and my own. I won't be friends with you—why didn't you help my mother?"

"I did . . . I . . . offered to marry her."

"So you knew she was pregnant?"

"Yes, well, she did tell me. When she told me . . . I offered to marry her. She was a lovely girl . . . though not as fine as you."

"You offered to marry her? You're lying!"

He gestured for her to keep her voice down. But she was feeling bold. She didn't care.

"How could you, you were married already?"

"Well, no . . . not quite. You see, I was only engaged to another girl. I could . . . I offered . . ."

"Then why didn't you marry her?" she insisted brutally.

"Her father . . . it's your mother's father . . . You see," said he, leaning his head to one side humbly, "I am Jewish. He didn't want his daughter to marry a Jew."

"You are Jewish!" exclaimed Malison. "I am Jewish too, then."

He nodded resignedly and sponged his face again. He looked very uncomfortable. Even though the top button of his shirt was undone, he felt constricted. He sponged his neck. Large dark rings underlined his armpits.

Malison was off balance for a few minutes. "My father is Jewish—what of it? What does it change? Why can't I kill a Jew? He ruined my mother's life—my life." The man sensed her hesitation and tried to take advantage of it.

"Look, Malison, what has happened has happened—many years ago. Let me do what I can to repair it—I'd love you to meet my family. My nice wife—" He quickly checked himself. "Not as nice or pretty as your mother, but nice—and I have two daughters and a son. You should meet them . . . they'll welcome you as a sister. Of course, money is difficult . . . hmm—there's nothing I can do there. I am not a rich man."

"No!" Malison shouted violently. "I don't want to meet your nice wife and your nice children, and I have not come for money. I loathe you, because you have ruined my mother's life and my own. I had ticks and fleas as a child and was made to sleep with the animals on filthy straw, because I am a bastard—and my fiancé wasn't allowed to see me again when his mother found out that I was a bastard. You did that to me. You—you—you! Why should I meet your nice wife and your nice children?"

"Please . . . please," he pleaded, "not so loud. Yes, I see . . . I see . . . I'm sorry. Perhaps I could do something. I could give something after all, every year. Are you continuing your studies or are you working in a shop?" he asked, seeing her shabby clothes.

"I pay my way through university myself, with my ironing," she answered proudly. "I don't want your money, I already told you!"

She knew she was angry at him not only because of what he had inflicted on her mother and on herself, but because he was so meek, because he offered no resistance, he was ready to comply, to accommodate, because he was indifferent to the suffering he had caused, and also because he was not a rogue. He was not a scoundrel, he was not dashing and daring, just inescapably mediocre. He was not the father she had dreamed of, hated, and adored secretly. She thought bitterly that he wasn't even worth killing.

He had been thinking about something too, for a while. He said, "Your mother–does she know you came to see me?"

"No, she doesn't know. She would have told me not to."

"Yes, it's better that way. You won't tell her, then?" And he was obviously afraid that she would.

"No, it would upset her too much," she said.

"Yes, much better–much better that way."

It was clear that he was wondering what to do next, how to get out of this situation, how to make sure that this scene would not be repeated. His card–his business card, that was it. He hoped that this was the right move–she seemed calmer now.

He fumbled in his pockets for something, produced a ten-thousand-lira note, decided it wasn't enough in the circumstances, and searched again. He half raised himself to dig deeper in his pocket, and as he did so his eyes caught sight of a young woman who was entering the lobby.

At that moment he was conscious of making a mistake, but he couldn't help himself. He searched his pocket for another ten thousand lire and his business card, while his eyes were fixed on the pretty woman. He thought, "Just the kind of high buttocks that I like, and she's got breasts too–I really must get myself a wallet, it is essential to have things handy." It took a long time, during which he sensed, rather than saw, that Malison had pulled the gun out of her basket. Although he was totally certain of this, he couldn't turn around, but kept following the lovely curves on the young woman's body as she was undulating across the lobby toward the desk.

Then it went very fast—a shattering explosion—a brutal jolt, something violent had thrown him backward—an excruciating pain in his eyes—a terrible mess of destruction of his face—all at once—screams—heat—sticky liquid. "Is this my blood?" One nagging thought persisted: "Something vitally important, neglected . . . Perhaps it is not too late . . . too late . . . too late. . . ."